DAYLE SMITH, MAUREEN TAYLOR
AND ARTHUR H. BELL

Why Should I?

Ten Keys to Motivating People

Lexingford Publishing

New York
Hong Kong
London

L

www.lexingfordpublishing.yolasite.com

ISBN: 0-98449382-4
ISBN-13: 978098449382-1
LCCN: 2010908291

DEDICATION

For Dayle M. Smith and Arthur Bell, dedicated with love to our children Art Jr., Lauren, and Maddie. For Maureen Taylor, dedicated to my family: Renn, Alexandra and Will. They always motivate me to be better.

Contents

Acknowledgements

The authors gratefully acknowledge not only the advice and perspectives of their academic mentors and colleagues at Harvard University, University of Southern California, Georgetown University, University of San Francisco, and San Francisco State University, but also the generosity of practicing executives, managers, and other employees at all levels who shared their experiences, thoughts, and feelings during the research period leading to the writing of this book. We especially express appreciation to consummate professionals at Google, eBay, Facebook, TRW, Lockheed Martin, McAfee, Wells Fargo Bank, Charles Schwab, New York Life, PriceWaterhouse Coopers, Cushman Wakefield, the U.S. State Department, Cisco, Oracle, Microsoft, Yahoo, SAP, Lucasfilm, Johnson & Johnson, the U.S. Coast Guard, American Stores, Safeway, and other organizations with which we have worked.

Note: all names, places and incidents used in scenarios and examples within this book are purely hypothetical and invented by the authors. Any resemblance to actual people, places, or incidents is entirely coincidental.

Introduction

Motivation? Let's start with you. You're considering whether to read this book. We, the authors, want to motivate you to do so.

But where does such motivation begin?

With you and your needs. To do your job well and create your own professional future, you may need to build a fire under those you supervise or members of your team.

Or you may be struggling with your own feelings of business stagnation and boredom. Monday morning meetings tell you that things just aren't right with your worklife. You may need to find a way to motivate yourself.

In either case, you want to know how to rekindle *enthusiasm* for professional opportunities and responsibilities. You want your employees to *want* to, not have to. You want more than their punched time-card. You want them to give their commitment and effort to their job. You probably want the same things for yourself.

This book provides proven answers for the question, 'How do I motivate myself and others?' Here we gather the brightest and best ideas on motivation from successful managers, winning companies, and academic research. We are confident that you will find in these "ten keys to motivation" a number of ways to convert chuggers into chargers.

In this short book, you will meet ten people who struggle with motivation problems. By analyzing their work attitudes and experiences, we can custom fit motivational keys, principles and plans to resolve their lackluster approach to work. We're betting that among these ten invented but true-to-life scenarios you will find several that shed light on what to do about motivational problems you're experiencing. Each "key" concludes with a quick summary of Management Tips you can put to work on the job right away.

That's our pitch and promise: read this book with care to understand how to motivate a wide variety of people in the workplace. One bonus: in discovering how to motivate others, you will probably find surefire ways to motivate yourself.

Key One

Motivation by Expectation

Our efforts intensify to the extent that we believe goal-fulfillment to be possible.

Todd M., 40, sells heavy industrial equipment for a major industrial broker on the West Coast. He is married without children and travels two weeks a month on average.

"My job is pretty much like Las Vegas: you spin the wheel and hope for a major score. If it doesn't come, you spin again. And you keep spinning, as long as it takes.

"When I started in this position six years ago, I got discouraged too easily. I remember one time in particular. I flew all the way up to Seattle from L.A. to meet a prospective customer. The guy had me spend most of the day with him going around to different job sites and looking at various pieces of equipment he already owned. It was typical Seattle weather—cold rain—and I came back with the flu.

"All for nothing. He bought from my competitor the next day for the same price I was offering him. I just about quit that day.

"But then there are the good days, when orders and commissions come in one on top of the other. Those are the days that keep me going.

"Now my philosophy is this: get out there and put in the legwork meeting new customers and understanding their operations. Eight contacts out of ten may lead nowhere, but if the remaining two pan out, it's fat city on payday.

"Traveling around as I do, I hear about job possibilities with other companies. But the reason I stay here is the upside potential. What else could I be doing that would net me well into the six figures in a good year?

"I tell the new salespeople that there's only one trick to having a really good year: avoid the post-honeymoon syndrome. This is when you wine and dine a new customer to the point of his or her first purchase or two, then gradually lose interest as you pursue other new customers. Customers are never 'in the bag,' I tell our sales force, and you should treat them as if they were.

"Since I'm the senior person now and usually hit the top sales numbers each year, the company is having me do some of the sales training for the new guys. It cuts into my own calls a bit, but I enjoy talking about something I know so well. And, although the company doesn't know it, I'm going to hit them up one of these days for a bonus based on the gross sales figures of the people I train. Why not? I've given them the secrets for their success."

Follow-up Information

Todd M. is under treatment for a chronic ulcer condition. He worries privately that his health won't sustain a continuing schedule of heavy travel. His company, however, has been holding him up lately as a model of sorts for the rest of the sales staff. Todd wonders what lies ahead for him in his later forties and fifties. He would like to have a plan for his life, but the ulcer situation has raised many unanswered questions.

"I'd rather burn out than rust out," Todd tells himself. He has not followed his doctor's advice to reduce stress levels in his professional life.

Motivators at Work

One important goal for Todd M. is making the sale. His Physiological Needs (food, shelter, clothing), economic security, social relations, sense of esteem, and other factors all depend in large part on his ability to close the deal.

To achieve this end, Todd is willing to engage in a period of goal-directed activity. Note that this activity (which can include business travel, product presentations, phone calls, and so forth) does not in itself fulfill Todd's needs as listed above. In fact, if he were only to engage in goal-directed activities without ever achieving the goal, he would be looked upon as a failure—a well-intentioned, hardworking but unsuccessful salesperson.

Early in his career, Todd perceived the relation of his goal-directed activities to goal fulfillment in this way:

goal-directed activities———-——- GOAL-FULFILLMENT ACTIVITIES

At this initial stage of his career, he simply couldn't bear to put in too much legwork (goal-directed activity); he had to see "results" (goal fulfillment) to keep his confidence up.

With experience, however, Todd now is content with a different allocation of goal-directed activity to goal fulfillment. In other words, he is more sure of his eventual success and therefore is willing to undergo periods of goal-directed activity without actual goal fulfillment, depicted as follows:

GOAL-DIRECTED ACTIVITIES———-——goal-fulfillment activities

Todd's hard-won sense of patience and confidence can be attributed in part to the powers of visualization and memory. Todd carries within himself influential memories about past sales he has made. He remembers holding large commission checks in his hand. He recalls the loud applause he received when he was recognized as Salesperson of the Year for the company. He sees the sales achievement plaques decorating his office wall.

In all these ways, Todd participates in *imaginative* goal fulfillment during goal-directed activity. This is not to say that imaginative goal fulfillment pays the mortgage. Todd realizes that dreaming about a big sale is the not the same thing as closing the actual deal. In a now-famous budget confrontation with California professors, then Governor Jerry Brown told professors seeking a pay raise that they should consider themselves paid in "psychic dollars" due to the relative prestige and social privilege of their positions. One professor then inquired if his state taxes could be paid in those same psychic dollars.

Todd M.'s motivation, in sum, is based largely on his expectations. The Expectancy Theories of motivation maintain that most of our actions are based not on receiving actual rewards or avoiding actual pain but instead on our expected (i.e., imagined) versions of these positive or negative payoffs.

Our efforts to succeed intensify to the extent that we believe goal-fulfillment to be possible. If Todd sniffs out a possible sale, he will "go for it" with all his energy. But as soon as he concludes that the sale is not possible (perhaps because of a competitor's lower bid), he may withdraw his efforts completely.

What motivates Todd, in a word, is the chase. David C. McClelland and John W. Atkinson studied this phenomenon across industries and employment levels. Contrary to intuition, they discovered that motivation does not continue to increase as the probability of goal-fulfillment nears 100 percent. In fact, as goal-fulfillment seems more and more a "sure thing," motivation tends to slack off. McClelland and Atkinson describe this pattern in their famous "50 Percent Curve." Motivation is near zero if there is no chance of success, but rises steadily as the chances for success improve. Interestingly, around the mid-point of 50 percent likelihood of success, motivation begins to dip. In fact, when the chances of success are practically 100 percent, motivation has fallen back to the zero point. In short, we feel no motivation when "it's a sure thing." Motivation rises as goal-fulfillment moves from improbable toward probable, but then begins to fall as goal-fulfillment begins to seem inevitable.

Members of a football team, for example, play their hearts out as long as the outcome is undecided. But as soon as failure or success is guaranteed, players may simply go through the motions of the sport.

In Todd M.'s words, this is the "post-honeymoon syndrome"—the dip in motivation after the courtship has won the prize. As Todd tries to teach his protégés, this syndrome can be resisted by recognizing it and redoubling efforts past the 50 percent point.

Also important to remember is that what you expect or what motivates you may be quite different in degree and type from what motivates others. Take the runners in the New York City marathon. The handful of world-class runners among the group may be motivated by the realistic expectation of winning fame and a large cash prize. But what of the thousands of also-rans in the race? What motivates them? Some expect to beat their own previous best times. That expectation is challenge enough to motivate their best performance. Others expect to be seen by friends and family. Still others expect only to finish the race and get the t-shirt.

In each case, what seems to be an obvious general expectation—winning the race—has in fact been individualized to a wide variety of sub-expectations. As a manager you can use expectancy theory best when you recognize that "obvious" expectations for the group aren't obvious at all when you get to know what individuals actually expect of themselves.

Victor Vroom has helped a generation of managers understand the inner workings of expectancy motivation. Vroom points out that expectancy involves three key factors:

If you believe that your effort affects your performance
(and)
If you believe that your performance determines predictable outcomes
(and)
If you believe that you value those outcomes

…Then you will be motivated to expend maximum or near-maximum effort to achieve the outcome.

In Todd's case, he first expects that his personal investment of energy (in the form of sales visits, travel, phone calls, and so forth) will affect his performance as a salesperson. "No one has success just handed to him," Todd likes to say. Second, he expects that his performance will lead to predictable outcomes. His contract with the company, for example, specifies that he will be paid a certain commission rate per sale. Finally, Todd knows that he values both the financial rewards and the prestige of being a top salesperson.

But remove any one of Vroom's three components and motivation evaporates. Let's say, for example, that Todd felt his sales were a matter of luck, not effort. Or imagine that the company simply wouldn't pay him his earned commission. In either case,

Todd's motivation to work would virtually disappear. Finally, imagine that Todd (perhaps because of some spiritual conversion) eschews money, the material world, and all its trappings. If work outcomes lose their meaning for Todd, motivation to achieve them ceases entirely.

This is precisely the motivational sinkhole into which many urban employees find themselves sinking. Their ostensible rewards—a salary, let's say, of $100,000 per year—ceases to have meaning as housing costs skyrocket along with other cost-of-living expenses. The reward aspect of the green paper symbols received in the pay envelope begins to pale as these dollars buy less and less satisfaction in terms of life style.

Employers in less commercially intense regions have learned to capitalize on this reality for motivational purposes. "Come to Kansas," one employment ad reads, "where a good salary still buys a great house in a safe city." As economic imbalances increase among regions, many employees find themselves trapped beneath an area's reward ceiling. A talented agricultural chemist in Montana can't afford to accept his company's offer of a transfer to the home office in New York City. His spacious home and other amenities in Montana couldn't be recreated in New York City for twice or three times his salary.

One final aspect of expectancy theory involves the availability of necessary environmental factors. I can believe that my effort to sell freezers to Eskimos will affect my sales performance; and I can believe that my company will indeed pay me for every freezer sold; finally, I can believe that I'd love to have those dollars. But if the subzero environment makes freezers unnecessary, my motivational supports fall like a house of cards.

Entrepreneurs often face this motivational Waterloo. Without adequate market studies, they assemble a ground-floor staff and set off with great enthusiasm to franchise the world (or some other sales goal). When the enterprise fails to achieve expected results, the boss too often—and incorrectly—examines only the three motivational components: Why aren't my employees giving their best? (the effort-performance component). Do I have to increase salaries and commissions? (the performance-outcomes component). Do they want something besides money? (the outcomes-value component).

The culprit all along may be availability. The region or economy may be to blame, not the motivational level or sincerity of the employees. A CEO's dollars, in other words, should sometimes be spent in market research and development rather than in employee pep talks.

Todd M.'s boss, for example, may soon have to confront a specialized case of availability with regard to Todd's chronic ulcer condition. No matter what Todd's expectations, his health may prove to be a limiting factor to his further achievement. Recognizing this, Todd's boss may opt to use Todd's expertise for in-house training rather subjecting him to the continuing rigors of the road.

In doing so, Todd's boss will have to walk an interesting motivational tightrope. Todd, after all, expects his performance to lead to valuable outcomes. To date, Todd has defined those valuable outcomes in terms of dollars and prestige as a top sales-person. Todd's boss will have to convince Todd that an increase in his prestige (his visibility in-house as the ultimate model of a salesperson) more than makes up for a dip in his economic rewards.

In summary, anything is possible in Todd's future, lim-ited only by his health. His motivation to work depends directly upon his expectations, which may be fulfilled by the company in both tangible and intangible ways. In short, we work because we believe, not necessarily because we receive.

Management Tips

Expectancy theories of motivation emphasize the inter-nal world of hopes and dreams more than the external world of money and position. Four practical lessons can be drawn from the Todd M. case:

1. Each individual has his or her own set of expectations and beliefs regarding work. These inner forces are their prime motivators for achievement.

2. Managers should not assume that external symbols of value (a high salary, a company car, and so forth) automatically have personal motivating value for a particular employee.

3. Managers choose motivators based on their knowledge of employees' personal expectations.

4. Managers guard against fall-offs in motivation particularly at the beginning of unpromising tasks and toward the conclusion of sure-bet tasks.

Key Two

Motivation by Understanding What People Need

We *all have an inborn order, or hierarchy, for what we want and need.*

Sandra R., 33, has worked for a large Midwestern chemical company for four years. She is divorced and has one child, Tammy, age 5.

"When I'm asked what I need from work, I usually say, 'Money, and more of it.' And that's partly true, as a single parent with sole responsibility for raising my daughter. But money isn't the whole story.

About five years ago, just after my daughter was born, I had what could be called a sick divorce. I was so miserable in my marriage that I signed anything and everything over to my husband just to get him out of the house and out of my life.

What I was left with was a transportation car, the apartment furniture, a big VISA bill, and a daughter to raise alone. I had about $600 in savings and no job.

So when I applied to this company as a secretary, it was literally to keep a roof over our heads and food on the table. I remember holding my first paycheck and crying in the restroom for relief and joy. We wouldn't starve. We would get by.

A few months later, Tammy came down with bronchitis. It was nothing that serious, but we went through a lot of medical tests and several prescriptions. I learned how to make the most of my medical insurance from work. And I realized that I could get sick for a day or a week and our world wouldn't collapse. I could go to the dentist, I could take Tammy, and insurance would pay most of it. I had life insurance and a retirement plan. For the first time in months, I felt safe for both of us.

Work became a big part of my social life. I don't know how it is in other companies, but in mine you pretty much hang out with employees at your same level. I'm friendly with my supervisor and her boss, but they usually have their own circle for lunch and after-work drinks.

My group is what we jokingly call the 'S.S.'—Satisfied Secretaries. You see, there are two basic groups of secretaries in the company. There are the 'wilders,' who seemingly have no responsibilities. A lot of them are just out of school or going part-time, still living at home or off Mom and Dad in some other way, with no kids to provide for and a party every other night. This group hates work, and at lunchtime and breaks they say so over and over. They're funny. Nothing at work is ever right for them. 'The temperature in the office is too hot (or cold).' 'The parking lot doesn't have enough lights.' 'The cafeteria coffee is awful.' You name it.

Then there's my group. I wouldn't say we love work, but we all rely on our jobs to keep our families going. I have nothing against the other group of secretaries, but I'm not 18 anymore and I can't pretend I am.

A year ago something good happened to me at work. I was promoted to executive assistant, which is one step up from secretary and pays more money. The company actually gave me business cards with my new title; I use them for salespeople, suppliers, and others I have to deal with.

I think I can be happy in this position for a long time. My parents are obviously proud of my promotion and feel that their daughter has finally succeeded at something. I've gotten to know most of the other executive assistants in my division, and some of us have started doing things after work.

There's no aspect of my present job that I can't handle and my work evaluations are excellent. Sometimes my boss asks me to take on projects for her that are out of my league, and I tell her so. I'd rather do my own work well than take on someone else's and do a mediocre job. It took a while, but think my boss understands that about me."

Follow-up Information

According to her supervisors, Sandra has the intelligence to move into training for a supervisory position. When approached with this idea, Sandra tends to pass it off as a compliment but an impractical option. She explains her negativity on the basis of her lack of a college degree. Other supervisors, she says, have more education that she does and she would feel out of place. This issue is not an obstacle on the part of the company, which is willing to pay for her tuition at night school to complete her degree. Sandra recently talked her daughter Tammy out of taking gymnastics classes after school: "You might get hurt, honey."

Motivators at Work

Sandra's changing work experience demonstrate what psychologist Abraham Maslow has called a "hierarchy of needs." In Maslow's view, we all have an inborn order, or hierarchy, for what we want. We move through stages of need, progressing to later stages only when earlier stages have been satisfied.

In commonsense terms, a "hierarchy of needs" simply means that we each have rather predictable priorities. We can call this order our List of Needs. If we're desperately hungry, for example, we will often risk our security to get food. But once we've eaten, new priorities assert themselves. We care more for our security, social relations, and other higher level needs.

Self-Actualization
Esteem
Social
Security
Physiological

These priorities are represented, from "lowest" (most basic, at the bottom of the list) to "highest" (most sophisticated, at the top of the list) in the following pages. As we discuss each need level in turn, we will capitalize the need we are emphasizing at the moment.

When Sandra first came to work, her structure of needs could well be depicted as the traditional list presented above. The most basic, bottom-of-the-list necessity, Physiological Needs, represents what was most important to Sandra at the time: her need to pay the rent and buy food for herself and her child. For the first few months of employment, Sandra was probably motivated to perform well primarily by her fear of not meeting these physiological needs.

For this reason, many companies have 60 to 90-day probation periods at the beginning of a person's employment. This policy acts as a not-so-subtle reminder that employment can come to a sudden halt, at the employer's unfettered discretion, during this try-out period. During her first weeks on the job, Sandra made it a point to get to work on time, abide by break time-limits, keep her nose to the grindstone primarily because she "really needed this job" and didn't want to get fired.

But notice what happens to the List of Needs once Sandra has become more sure she can pay her bills for food and shelter. As her worries about meeting basic physiological needs subside, a new set of needs take prominence in her mind and behavior: these are Security Needs.

Self-Actualization
Esteem
Social
SECURITY
Physiological

Sandra's security needs, as shown by the capitalization in the List of Needs, begin to focus on the many 'what ifs' of life: What if my child gets sick? What if I need expensive dental care? What if my car breaks down? With such thoughts in mind, Sandra is in the grip of Security Needs as her primary motivators. Her benefits package at work looms large to her as a main reason why she works well and hard. Notice that as long as this set of Security Needs predominates in her thinking, other motivators—a classier job title, for example, or even a higher salary at another company—would not appeal to her unless they were accompanied by a comparable or better benefits package to assuage her Security Needs.

Let's allow a few months to pass. Sandra has now become confident that her basic Security Needs, like the Physiological Needs before them, will continue to be met. She doesn't worry about having the money for health or dental care. (This is not to say that such needs disappear for her entirely; they simply become less dominant in the hierarchy of needs that motivate her.)

Now Social Needs exert themselves more forcefully in Sandra's thinking and feeling. She finds real pleasure in her work friendship with the "satisfied secretaries" group. She says that she wouldn't quit her job for a modest pay raise elsewhere because "I would miss the people." In short, a new emphasis now appears in her List of Needs:

Self-Actualization
Esteem
SOCIAL
Security
Physiological

To satisfy her social needs, Sandra has not made friendships randomly at work. By seeking and finding membership in the "satisfied secretaries" circle, she has located a group that supports her values and shares many of her life experiences. She doesn't make close friends among the younger, party set of secretaries. Her Social Needs can be fulfilled only when she finds others who understand and generally approve her day-to-day life choices.

Once she has satisfied her Social Needs, Sandra moves on to a new set of motivating interests: her need for Esteem. Foremost in her mind at this stage are questions about her relative prestige in the eyes of people who matter to her: What do Mom and Dad think about her position at work and recent promotion? How does her daughter Tammy feel about Mommy's job? For that matter, what does Sandra herself think about her professional status and future? Is this secretarial job "it" for her? Her List of Needs during this stage can be represented as follows:

Self-Actualization
ESTEEM
Social
Security
Physiological

While influenced primarily by Esteem Needs, Sandra can be motivated by anything, however trivial, that supports her status—a business card, a nameplate on her desk, a slightly augmented job title. Banks are notorious among major industries for using the Esteem Needs of its employees to take the place of paying higher salaries. The prospect of earning the title "Branch

Vice President" can be extremely motivating to an employee, even when accompanied by little or no salary improvement.

Notice, however, that Sandra's primary motivators can easily flip back to the Social Needs level. For example, if Sandra's main social group at work felt that she was snubbing them in pursuit of status and titles, there's a good chance that Sandra would delay or ignore her Esteem Needs until repairing her social relationships. In actual fact, many employees pass up the chance to become a manager if such a promotion means they must supervise (and perhaps alienate) their friends.

Like Sandra, many rising professionals find themselves oscillating stressfully between the levels of Social Needs and Esteem Needs. New job titles often bring a new set of day-to-day acquaintances and friendships at work. Sandra, for example, has lunch more often with other executive assistants once she has been promoted to that job category. She probably reassures her earlier social set at work that "I really miss all of you" and "we'll have to get together soon to catch up." She may explain away her new lunch and after-work commitments on the basis of work responsibilities: "All the executive assistants have to get together for lunch pretty often to compare notes on what's going on."

The truth, of course, is that Sandra is trying to harmonize her Social Needs with her Esteem Needs. In making new friendships while attempting to hold on to older ones, she is building a social life that does not interfere with her growing need to make people proud of her, and to be proud of herself.

So let's say that Sandra succeeds in satisfying her Esteem Needs in coordination with her supportive social network. She is now has the relative luxury to move on to the motivating influence of Self-Actualization Needs, as represented in this emphasis within the List of Needs:

SELF-ACTUALIZATION
Esteem
Social
Security
Physiological

At this stage, she confronts such questions as "What is my life about?" and "Is this what I really want to be doing?" She cares intensely in this frame of mind about her competence and personal achievements, past, present, and especially future. She focuses on her skills not to impress others but fulfill her own need for a sense of expertise and control. She craves a high score not on anyone else's measurement scale, but rather on her own personal chart of what she knows she can do.

In seeking self-actualization, Sandra sets her sights on tasks and relationships that are within what she perceives as her scope of possibility. She will reject projects and opportunities that she defines as "just not me" (that is, out of sync with her general sense of self-actualizing options). On the other hand, she will also reject projects and opportunities that seem beneath her.

In a fascinating experimental validation of Sandra's situation, Harvard psychologist David C. McClelland asks participants to throw rings over a peg from any distance they chose.

Obviously a person could get all the rings onto the peg by standing right over it. By contrast, a person might never get a single ring onto the peg by standing too far away from it. The vast majority of participants instinctively sought out their own "interest range"—that is, the distance away that promised some success but also involved challenge and risk.

In the case of Sandra in this chapter, she has chosen to "throw her rings" from a very close distance. She regularly turns down project opportunities from her boss because they "aren't in my league." Sadly, her self-imposed limitations are being passed along to her daughter, with reference to the chance to take gymnastics classes: "You might get hurt, honey."

As Sandra's employer, you may regret the low ceiling of achievement under which Sandra has chosen to lead her professional life. The question is how you can raise that ceiling—in effect, how you can help Sandra find pleasure in higher levels of achievement—without arousing unmanageable levels of insecurity within her: "My boss isn't satisfied with me" (worries about Esteem Needs); "If I fail everyone will mock me" (worries based on Esteem and Social Needs), and so forth.

In your efforts to motivate an employee like Sandra, keep in mind the rings-and-peg experiment. Your goal is to help Sandra find excitement in moving back farther and farther from the peg—that is, allowing herself to take on progressively greater challenges. All the while, however, she must have a relatively secure sense of her competence and ability to succeed; she has to ring the peg often. In practical terms, therefore, you would ease Sandra into new job tasks gradually. You would remind her about accomplishments in new areas and emphasize achievements rather than failure. You would highlight the excitement of new challenges in such a way that does not arouse her fears of losing her social connections or risking embarrassing failure.

Management Tips

Several insights for managers emerge from an understanding of the List of Needs.

1. Motivators have meaning only in relation to the strength of a given need as perceived by the individual employee. At some stages, the lure of money may be almost meaningless; at other stages, it may seem all-important.

2. Managers can understand their employees' needs only by listening to and observing them.

3. Employees will take on new challenges only when their other needs remain relatively satisfied. The increased status of new job responsibilities and titles may be unattractive to employees concerned primarily about social needs.

4. Managers tend to project their own stage of need onto their employees. A manager obsessed with upper levels of self-actualization, for example, may not understand why subordinates resist attending a two-week seminar on advanced technical skills. Don't they want to be more competent than their coworkers? Don't they want to master sophisticated skills? Perhaps not, at least from the point of view of the workers themselves. These opportunities may be motivating for managers who have already satisfied other levels of need, but not for subordinates who are still struggling to satisfy those needs.

Key Three
Motivation by Fairness

We compare what we do and receive with what others do and receive.

Peggy Woodward, 35, is one of six mid-level mangers in the San Francisco office of a commercial credit firm. She is single and has sole caregiving responsibility for her elderly mother.

"Am I getting what I deserve at this company? Yes and no.

"Yes, for my education, which is a B.A. in Business Administration from Ohio State, and my level of work experience. I'm getting a better-than average salary for this industry. The benefits package is good and we have a profit-sharing plan that adds a few thousand dollars to my retirement plan each year.

"But no, I'm not getting what I deserve when it comes to this specific office and some of the things that have been happening here. Last month, for example, all six of us in the mid-level management range found out about our raises: a five percent rise for each of us across the board.

I went home stunned that day. Any objective observer of the company would have seen that, over the past year, four of us have been working like dogs and that two—I'll call them Alice and Ruth—have been absolutely loafing.

"Last year my immediate boss, the vice president of cost accounting, gave us all a sermon about merit raises—how we would individually be rewarded for our efforts. Like fools, four of us took that message seriously. We came in early, left late, often skipped lunches, and even spent some Saturdays on the job. We took on a lot of extra projects we didn't have to.

"Alice and Ruth, however, found every excuse in the book to be away from their desks. They each took their maximum number of sick days, got permission to attend off-site management seminars in fancy locations, and generally treated their jobs as a hobby. On several occasions, Ruth's subordinates came to me for information and decisions that she was responsible for.

The four of us have agreed that, if the company won't reward our efforts, we won't give it. Alice and Ruth have apparently set the standard of what it takes to get a five percent raise here, and that's the standard that the four of us are going to follow as well.

"I'm not coming in to work a minute before eight and I'm leaving promptly at five, no matter what needs doing. If the vice president asks me about my change in work habits, I'll be more than happy to explain—and I'll have three others managers there to back me up.

"Either Alice and Ruth have to start pulling their weight around here, or the company should reward those of us who do.

Follow-up Information

Peggy W. and her mother are active church members. Although she has many friends, Peggy considers her own social and romantic life on hold so long as her mother needs care. Last year, Peggy underwent psychological treatment for anxiety-induced panic disorder. With the help of medication and breathing exercises, she has been able to control this condition. She is an avid gardener. "We have the only lawn on the street with absolutely no crab grass," she says with pride.

Motivators at Work

Consider Peggy W.'s point of view. She has no complaints about her salary or benefits per se; in fact, she admits they are better than average for her industry. Nor does she dislike her work tasks in themselves.

What bedevils her is the mismatch between her effort/reward ratio and the effort/reward ratios of some of her peers in the company. She is losing motivation, in other words, because of what she perceives as a fundamental lack of fairness.

This problem of perceived inequity plagues many organizations in their hiring and compensation decision. Let's say a business school hired new PhD instructors in the 1980s for $40,000 per year. The salaries of these men and women have risen year by year, according to the school's pay schedule, so that by 2010 they were earning $105,000 on average. But when the school goes out to hire new PhD instructors in 2010, it finds that due to market condition these people cannot be attracted to teach for less than $120,000.

The result is both obvious and interesting. The school does go ahead and hire the $120,000 per year PhD instructors—it can hardly do otherwise if it intends to staff its program—but it does not alter the pay scale of those instructors who have labored at the school for decades under a lower salary schedule. This mismatch in salary between high-priced newcomers and bargain-basement oldtimers is a guaranteed formula for fairness disputes among the workforce.

"I've given my work life to this place," one employee complains, "and now I find out that
I'm earning twenty percent less than a new employee. The company had better not expect much from me in the future. I'm going to start treating the company like it's treating me!"

J. Stacy Adams is the father of equity theories of motivation. Inevitably, he says, we compare what we do and receive with what others do and receive. If we feel an inequity as a result of that comparison, that response can become a powerful factor in determining our own motivational levels. As in the case of Peggy W., few other traditional motivators—salary, reputation, meaningful work—can overcome the deep burn that we feel because of perceived inequity.

Adams' equation for equity is straight-forward:

$$\frac{\text{My reward}}{\text{my input}} \text{ should equal} \frac{\text{your reward}}{\text{your input}}$$

When the sides of the equation balance, we're satisfied and proceed to respond to our usual set of motivators. But when the balance tilts heavily against us, we often act out our frustration and sense of injustice.

These responses can take several forms to restore the balance of the equation. First, we may decide to reduce our input (our effort, involvement, or leadership) to produce what we consider a more equitable effort/reward ratio, and perhaps to "pay back" those who caused the felt inequity in the first place. Second, we may try to make the effort/reward ratio more just by increasing the reward side. For example, we may ask for an increased salary, a better commission schedule, or a bonus in the form of money or privileges.

If we have success at neither of these balancing attempts, we may decide to wipe the board clean entirely by quitting. This action effectively takes us out of what we perceive as an inequitable comparison with others. We may also feel our resignation pays back those who caused the inequity; for a period of weeks or longer, they may have trouble filling our former spot and covering our duties. We imagine that they regret their inequitable actions.

Third, we can attempt to reestablish an equitable balance between ourselves and others by changing their side of the equation. We could insist, for example, that the other person work harder or receive less money. Fourth, we can attempt to substitute another ratio for the one we dislike. Instead of comparing ourselves disadvantageously to Person A in the company, we may switch our perspective entirely and begin comparing ourselves to Person B.

In Peggy W.'s case, for example, her company might decide to label the four hard-working managers as participants in the company's "fast track" program for rising managers. The other two managers would not be considered as fast-trackers. Although her salary, responsibilities, and raise have not changed a whit, Peggy is now content with the new arrangement; she compares herself only to the other three hard-working managers. That comparison, she feel, is equitable.

Finally, we can attempt to tilt the balance to the even point or even toward our favor by psychologically distorting the data used for comparison. Peggy, for example, might take an empathetic view of one manager's child-care responsibilities or another's need for further education. This new perspective may make her feel more content with the apparent imbalance in work and reward. Some theorists, however, argue that balance is still at issue: Peggy is saying to herself, in effect, that her own total pain for pay is less than or equal to another person's total pain for pay, when childcare difficulties or other matters are factored into the equation. In this version, Peggy just doesn't want anyone to have it easier than she does, with all factors being considered.

Another psychological distortion technique involves what Leon Festinger calls "cognitive dissonance." When our perceptions of the outer world support our perceptions of ourselves and our interests, these perceptions are said to be in a consonant relationship ("harmony," as it were). Peggy's perception of the three hard-working managers is consonant with her perception of her own role and value to the company. But Peggy's perception of the idle managers is dissonant with her perception of herself. She finds that she cannot simultaneously believe that she is being treated equitably and they are being treated equitably.

One common response to cognitive dissonance, Festinger points out, is to quit hearing in part or in full: Peggy may select only those aspects of an idle manager's work day that are consonant for her: "Well, she delegates well, and I guess that counts for something." Or Peggy may shut out all information from the dissonant source: "I don't want to hear about it. I get so angry. I just want to do my job and be left alone."

Or Peggy may respond to cognitive dissonance by practicing the psychological defense of disbelief. Festinger's research demonstrates that "heavy smokers are less likely to believe that there is a relationship between smoking and lung cancer than nonsmokers." In Peggy's case, she may choose not to believe what she hears about the idle managers. "I've heard the stories, but I'm sure they're not really getting away with half of what people say. It's all gossip and it doesn't bother me one bit."

Finally, what about the "up" side of the equity equation? How do we respond when we discover ourselves to be overpaid or overprivileged in comparison to our equally hardworking peers? Research is mixed. On one hand, studies point to corporate superstars who give of themselves in direct proportion to their pay. "Because I earn $395,000 a year here," one senior executive says, "I would be ashamed not to give the company at least a 50-hour week on average." On the other hand, there are studies of some tenured professors and other high-pay/high-security professionals that show a significant dip in productivity compared to the lower-pay/lower-security periods in their careers.

But one fact stands out incontrovertibly for those interested in motivation: when people feel they are the victims of inequity, they lose motivation to accomplish company goals. Interestingly, they may not lose motivation *per se*. An employee angered by felt inequity may be highly motivated to complain, join or organize support groups, and even vandalize company property or sabotage company projects.

Those who believe deeply in equity for all within an organization may wonder why organizations of all kinds—businesses, colleges, government bureaus—don't simply raise everyone's pay to maintain fair balance with the salaries of newcomers. In fact, such large-scale pay adjustments are rarely made by organizations. More commonly, employees realize that their "sign-on salary"— the amount they are willing to accept to begin the job—defines their pay contract with the company, even those raises may increase that salary somewhat each year. These employees realize that the company is free to go out and hire others for whatever it wishes. Fairness, in this context, is determined not by how my work and effort measure up against your work and effort, but instead by the inescapable fact that market conditions determined my worth at the time of hiring just as they determine the market worth (often higher) of newcomers to the organization.

Management Tips

Managers sometimes cause inequities by the way they distribute work and rewards. But just as often, as in the Peggy W. case, inequities develop as a result of worker attitudes and actions. No matter what the cause, perceived inequities can be minimized in these ways:

1. Managers should study their organizations to determine where equity comparisons are likely to be made.

2. Managers can influence equity comparisons by distinguishing job titles, job descriptions, chains of reporting, numbers of people supervised, and types of rewards (including "perks") distributed.

3. Managers can prevent some forms of equity comparison by restricting the amount or type of information available to employees about the total amount of work and rewards given to others.

4. Managers can reduce the negative impact of unavoidable inequities (as perceived) by the ethical use of expectation motivators. Employees who feel cheated in the short term may continue to work hard toward company goals if they have reasonable expectations of just rewards in the long term.

Key Four

Motivation by Work Attitudes

Key factors to employee motivation may lie within each employee, not in attractions from the outside world.

Richard Y., 25, is a systems analyst for a Miami computer company. In that capacity, he often accompanies salespeople on their calls and offers technical advice on what hardware and software customers should buy for specific applications. Richard is engaged to be married within a year.

"I have very strong opinions about my present job. Not that anyone in the company is listening. I expect to quit soon and probably will take a job with one of our competitors. If it weren't for the expenses of my upcoming marriage, I would probably be out the door of the company already.

"Here's what I face. This company is making money hand over fist, even in a slow economy. All our customers want to upgrade their computer equipment on a regular basis. Making sales is like shooting fish in a barrel. I walk into a client's office with a salesperson who usually knows next to nothing about computer systems but is personable and attractive. He or she introduces me as a computer expert. The client describes a computer problem of some kind and I recommend a solution. Usually it's a no-brainer, not because I'm so smart but because the client knows so little about computers.

"The company is getting rich on these kinds of easy sales. And what happens to the profits? In its infinite wisdom, the company's executive committee has decided to spend heavily on a 'stimulating work environment' for employees. So in my office I have a $2000 walnut desk, three leather chairs, and some original artwork on the walls. We have an expensive new 'dining lounge' instead of the old coffee room. We're driving BMWs instead of Chevrolets as our company cars. And thanks to the executive committee, I have a benefits plan that pays for anything, anytime, anywhere.

"Don't get me wrong. These fringe benefits are nice, and friends nearly keel over when they walk into my luxurious office. But all this pretty stuff doesn't change my opinion about my job.

"I'll tell you the truth. I think my company is under-utilizing me. I'm paraded around with salespeople like some kind of guru to utter a bit of techno-babble just to sell a client on an updated or expanded computer system. I think the company should be going after much bigger fish. I would love to get involved in a more complicated computer transaction for a large-scale government or corporate application. I'd like to really put my skills to work and be rewarded accordingly if I helped to land some big contracts.

"The company thinks it is making me happy by giving me thicker carpets and more flex-time. But they just don't understand that I'm getting no satisfaction from my work. I want to use my skills fully on the job. I don't like treading water, even in the executive Jacuzzi."

Follow-up Information

Richard Y. graduated with a B.S. in computer science from UCLA, with a GPA of 4.0. In his spare time, he experiments with new computer devices of his own invention. Richard keeps in touch with many of his college friends, some of whom are working in research positions for IBM, Oracle, and Apple. These friends rarely ask about Richard's job; Richard suspects that his friends feel he has "sold out" for work that is too easy for him.

Motivators at Work

As early as 1924, researchers interested in work efficiency hypothesized that many key factors to employee motivation lay primarily in the outside world, not within the individual worker. In that year, efficiency experts at Western Electric Company of Hawthorne, Illinois, began to study the effects of illumination on work productivity.

Following standard scientific methods, they selected a test group of employees and a comparable control group. Lighting in the work area occupied by the test group was gradually increased. As expected, the productivity of the test group rose as illumination increased.

But to the surprise of the researchers, the productivity of the control group also rose, even though no change at all had been made in the level of illumination in their work area.

These unusual results attracted the attention of Harvard's Elton Mayo. Over a period of two years, Mayo and his team tried all manner of workplace enhancements upon test groups—rest breaks, company-paid lunches, more comfortable work stations, and so forth. To their astonishment, control groups without these emoluments performed as well or better than the test groups. Finally, researchers took away all work enhancements from the test group and plunged them back to their original work conditions. Surely, researchers thought, we will now see productivity plunge, as workers react negatively to these changes.

Just the opposite occurred. Productivity for the test groups reached an all-time high.

From these famous experiments has come a term familiar to every social researcher: the Hawthorne Effect. Mayo and his team had discovered that any group singled out for special attention, even for control purposes, will usually respond by increased motivation. If only for a brief period, these selected workers feel themselves to be on stage, in the spotlight. They perform accordingly.

It is ironic, in fact, that these early studies of the physical workplace should give rise to the human relations movement in business and industry. The Hawthorne researchers had demonstrated that people make the difference in organization, seldom because of their physical surroundings and often in spite of them.

In the opening scenario of this chapter, Richard Y.'s company hasn't yet gotten the message implicit in the Hawthorne experiments. Richard's company is still trying to motivate him and other employees by creature comforts: nice offices, luxury cars, and the rest.

These workplace enhancements, in the language made famous by Frederick Herzberg, are *maintenance factors*. Herzberg also called them hygiene factors—conducive to good business health but not the cause of it.

In studying the nature of work motivation, Herzberg and his colleagues began by interviewing accountants and engineers from various companies. these people were asked two questions:

"Tell me about a time when you felt exceptionally good about your job."

"Tell me about a time when you felt exceptionally bad about your job."

After analyzing more than 4,000 responses to these questions, Herzberg and his team saw a clear pattern emerging. When people wanted to express satisfaction with their jobs, they listed a predictable handful of things they liked. Herzberg called these "satisfiers" or motivators. But when it came to expressing dissatisfaction with their jobs, people did not list the absence of satisfiers. Instead, they came up with a separate list of item Herzberg called "dissatisfiers" or maintenance factors.

Here, first, there are top six satisfiers identified by Herzberg's study:

- Achievement
- Recognition
- The work itself
- Responsibility
- Advancement
- Growth

By contrast, here are the top six dissatisfiers from the same study:

- Company policy and administration
- Supervision
- Relationship with supervisor
- Work conditions
- Relationships with peers
- Relationships with subordinates

In complaining about company policies and administration, interviewees pointed to missing or unfair grievance procedures, poor performance appraisal methods, rigid attendance rules, and impractical vacation schedules. Typical complaints about work conditions included safety hazards, claustrophobia from working in confined spaces, lack of personal comfort at work stations, noise levels, and air pollutants.

But if we solve any one of these factors what do we have? A motivated employee? Not at all, says Herzberg. His point is that what it takes to satisfy an employee's needs (i.e., motivate him or her) differs from what it takes to maintain a complaint-free or even praiseworthy work environment.

Put another way, a lousy work environment can lower motivation but a superb work environment alone can't create it.

Let's consider Richard Y. in relation to his company. Richard understands clearly what he wants from his company, and his "wish list" accords closely with Herzberg's "satisfiers." Richard wants to achieve up to his capacity, not tread water, even for attractive pay. He wants to extend his knowledge and skill through challenging work experiences. He wants recognition, perhaps most of all from his college buddies who have gone on to interesting work opportunities.

But instead of listening to Richard's list of satisfiers, his company has wrongly decided to eliminate any potential dissatisfiers. Probably without knowing anything about Herzberg's work, the company spent its time and money trying to remove any possible dissatisfiers in an effort to keep Richard motivated. Company policies were loosened to the point of *laissez faire* management. Supervision was both rare and gentle. Work conditions were glamorized by expensive offices and cars, and worker relationships were spiced by frequent office parties and get-away vacations.

But so what? Richard's eagerness to find other employment is eloquent testimony to the crucial difference between motivators (satisfiers) and mere maintenance factors.

Do We All Have the Same Motivators?

Periodically in recent decades, management experts Paul Hersey and Kenneth H. Blanchard have replicated a study first published in 1949 by Lawrence Lindahl. He set out to determine whether supervisors are motivated by the same things that motivate rank-and-file workers. The relative positions of importance assigned to ten motivators by supervisors and workers are shown here (1 = most wanted aspect of job):

Good working conditions: Supervisors rank as 4, workers rank as 9

Feeling "in on things": Supervisors rank as 10, workers rank as 2

Tactful disciplining: Supervisors rank as 7, workers rank as 10

Appreciation for work done: Supervisors rank as 8, workers rank as 1

Management loyalty to workers: Supervisors rank as 6, workers rank as 8

Good wages: Supervisors rank as 1, workers rank as 5

Promotion and growth within the company: Supervisors rank as 2, workers rank as 7

Understanding of personal problems: Supervisors rank as 9, workers rank as 3

Job security: Supervisors rank as 3, workers rank as 4

Interesting work: Supervisors rank as 5, workers rank as 6

The results in our day, report Hersey and Blanchard, have not changed substantially for managers and supervisors. "The only real changes," they write, "seem to be that workers, over the last five to ten years, were increasing in their desire for 'promotion and growth with the company' and 'interesting work.'" And, Hersey and Blanchard point out, in times of economic decline, workers again emphasize "good wages" and "job security."

The implications of these studies are important for both supervisors and workers. If you're a supervisor or manager, you may inadvertently select motivators for your workers based on your own list of high-priority motivators. Because a ten percent raise (your item #1) would send you over the moon with joy, you might assume that such a raise would prove similarly motivating to your entry level employees. But consider that "good wages" was no more than number 5 on their list of wants. Understandably, entry level workers raised from $8.15 per hour to $8.95 per hour (about a 10 percent increase) may not be instantly motivated to increase their productivity dramatically. A few, in fact, may yawn at the raise.

Recognizing crucial differences in motivation is more important than ever as organizations move toward global markets and diverse workforces. Without generalizing too broadly, it can be observed that in some Asian cultures workers opt for a less competitive environment in which all share in success rather than the more typically Western motivator of a trip to Tahiti for only the top sales reps. It would be wrong, of course, to attach a single motivational profile or strategy to any particular ethnic or cultural group. The point is simply this: workers in cultural minorities are often motivated in ways that may seem odd to the manager from the predominant culture in the company. Recognizing those differences in motivation is an important key to effective management, especially with a diverse workforce.

Management Tips

A clear understanding of the differences between motivators and maintenance factors helps managers select powerful motivators that connect with worker needs and desires.

1. In assessing motivational programs, managers should watch for the Hawthorne Effect. Any employee or group of employees highlighted for special attention will respond with temporarily increased productivity.

2. Dissatisfying work conditions can restrict the capacity of workers to perform and their motivation to do so.

3. The elimination of dissatisfying work factors does not automatically create a satisfying and motivating work climate.

4. Motivators (satisfiers) may be different for each individual. Managers have to understand an individual worker's wants in order to choose effective motivators.

5. Managers often have a set of motivators for themselves that differ significantly in priority from those of their workers. Managers should not impose their motivational priorities on others who may have quite different motivational needs.

Key Five
Motivation by Approval

What your employer thinks of you can be a powerful motivational force, for better or for worse.

Linda P., 36, has worked as a buyer for a chain of suburban Los Angeles clothing stories for four years. She is married with two children.

"I'll tell you what I've experienced at this company and what I know others have experienced. It's not a gender thing or a matter of race. But it's definitely a form of prejudice nonetheless.

"Two brothers own this company. Both are in their late 50s and they spend all day, every day, supervising us in the office. That's Supervise with a capital S.

"These bosses make it obvious what they think of their employees. In their eyes, we're all lazy or mischievous children that have to be watched, scolded, and nagged throughout the day. One or the other of them literally stands by the entrance door at 8:00 a.m. every morning to see who's exactly on time and who's a minute or two late. Believe me, if you're one of the unlucky people who come in at 8:05 or 8:10, you're going to get a very surly memo the next day. Lunches and breaks are the same story.

"I've worked in other companies, and I can assure you that these two bosses have nothing to complain about with their workers. Almost without exception, everyone here tries to do a good job and go the extra mile—but in spite of, not because of, the behavior of the bosses. We do have a lot of turnover, however. About every six weeks, someone seem to "get into it" with one of the two brothers, and then there's another empty desk.

"My husband and I often talk about why these two men act this way. I don't think they enjoy their work at all anymore, so they assume that their employees hate work as well. Their only feeble attempt at motivating us is the repeated promise of some kind of bonus if we can exceed our sales goals. In my four years here, I have seen only two yearly bonuses, both of them less than $3000.

"Let me give you two typical examples of what we're up against. Because of sudden resignations, a senior management slot opened up a month ago. We in the office had to read about the opening in the newspaper; the two brothers assumed that no one already on staff was bright enough or ambitious enough to be interested in the job.

"Then there are our irregular staff meetings. The two brothers chair the meeting and basically lecture us for two hours on how expenses are going up, shoplifters are supposedly everywhere, and we're not earning our salaries. Sometimes they open up a topic for discussion, but we've all learned never to suggest solutions to problems. The brothers consider themselves the only ones capable of solutions. Our job in discussion is just to fill out the details about the problem itself.

"Why do I stay? It's close to home, I have some seniority here, and my husband works in the same part of town. Would I like a better job, even at a lower salary? You bet...and I'm always looking."

Follow-up Information

Eight years ago, the two brothers who own Linda's company were victims of an elaborate embezzlement scheme by several key employees, some of whom the brothers had befriended. Their losses were never recovered, nor was their trust in employees generally. But no matter what the brothers' reasons for their management style, Linda feels stalled in her own development as a buyer. "I never get a chance to try out my ideas," she complains.

Motivators in Action

Imagine yourself a factory superintendent some two hundred years ago during the Industrial Revolution in England. You arrive at work to face a horde of laborers, most of them recently driven into the city by hunger and government agricultural "reforms." These men, women, and children are generally ill-fed, ill-clothed and ill-housed. They are ready to do virtually anything for a day's meager pay. But they have no skills. Few can even read. If given the chance, some will steal in their desperation.

How do you manage such a workforce? Elizabeth Gaskell describes the bleak beginnings of factory life in her novel, *North and South*. Later, Charles Dickens traces the sad social results of that system in *Hard Times*. Both novelists make clear how these workers were managed: like misbehaving animals.

The more polite term by the turn of the twentieth century had become the Rabble Hypothesis. The laboring masses were often viewed by industrialists and finance barons as virtual beasts of burden, to be driven by the whips of fear and held captive to employment by financial chokeholds. Managers were advised to rule with an iron fist: Drive up production by threatening workers with punishment and termination. Banish "trouble-makers" from employment at the first hint of objection. Hire and fire on the spot to match the ups and downs of business.

The human reaction eventually challenged such treatment, and immortal descriptions of that process lie at the heart of works like *The Grapes of Wrath* and *The Jungle*. But the Rabble Hypothesis did not disappear for managers.

According to Douglas McGregor, the rigid attitudes of many Industrial Revolution managers have simply been recast into new language and concepts for our own day. McGregor terms this new version of the Rabble Hypothesis the "Theory X" approach to management.

Notice in its tenets, as listed below, the remaining pessimism about human nature and motivation.

Theory X Management Principles

1. Most people hate work.
2. Most people want to avoid responsibility.
3. Most people have little ambition for themselves.
4. Most people prefer to be led.
5. Most people have little ability to solve problems.

6. Most people are motivated to work primarily for food, shelter, clothing, and security.

7. Most people require close control to prevent mistakes and prohibit loafing.

This is the work environment that appalls Linda P. She no doubt believes quite different things about herself in relation to her work than the views held by her bosses. Yet in frustration she also feels herself becoming in part the bitter, vindictive, and uncommitted employee her bosses treat her as. She feels she is gradually sinking to their level.

Social scientist Chris Argyris focused on this unfortunate aspect of poor management practices. In his view, many organizations are designed according to principles and assumptions that keep immature people from developing to their potential and, just as often, cause mature people like Linda P. to become, or at least act, in less mature ways.

Argyris's strongest argument against such management practices springs from his succinct description of human developmental stages. Left to our natural development from infancy to adulthood, he says, we human beings move from

- passivity to activity
- dependence to independence
- limited behaviors to complex behaviors
- flighty interests to profound, sustained interests
- "now" thinking to past/present/future perspectives
- subordinance to equality and leadership
- lack of self-awareness to selfhood and self-control

But too many organizations, Argyris finds, try to move us backward along this natural development path. Workers are often encouraged to be passive and accepting, to follow the leader unthinkingly, to restrict their attention to trivial problems, to leave long-range planning to the bosses, to accept perpetual subordination as their lot in life, and to put little stock in one's self. Workers are often viewed as just replaceable cogs within the company machinery.

Managers in these kinds of organizations, Argyris concludes, have no room to complain if their workers seem unmotivated and unresourceful. The very management structure of the company has created such slaves. Along the way, strong and independent selves like Linda P. probably left the company in droves. Just as Linda contemplates leaving her present employment, these talented workers feared eventually becoming the drones they were assumed to be by management. For both McGregor and Argyris, the alternative to "Theory X" management involves a liberalized view of human nature and behavior. In his description of "Theory Y" assumptions, McGregor looks toward a new generation of managers and new assumptions:

Theory Y Management Assumptions

1. Work can be an enjoyable as play.
2. Most people want to accept reasonable levels of responsibility.
3. Most people have strong goals for themselves, and seek organizations that can help them fulfill those goals.
4. Most people like to lead occasionally.
5. Most people are good problem-solvers.

6. Most people in a prosperous society are motivated by goals beyond basic food, shelter, and security.

7. Most people require no policing or close control by the organization to prevent them from stealing or loafing.

People treated by these assumptions will act accordingly, and the organization will be the beneficiary of their actions. Linda P., for example, would love to work in an environment where her creativity and ambition could take wing. In such an environment, it would be natural for Linda to stay late at work to finish up a stimulating project. The old factory concept of arriving "on time" or staying "over time" would give way to more flexible ideas of work scheduling.

Are any companies actually run according to Theory Y principles in the twenty-first century? Emphatically yes. The general rule is that companies in a seller's market for employees (a time when companies can't find all the talent they need) must employ at least some Theory Y principles to keep their workforce intact and motivated. No self-motivated adult, after all, willingly endures the kinds of belittling treatment the two brothers regularly dispensed on Linda and her coworkers. Examples of current companies with strong Theory Y management commitments are Levi Strauss, Genentech, Apple, Johnson & Johnson, IBM, Cisco Systems, and many others.

In summary, what your employer thinks about you can be a powerful motivational influence, for better or for worse. The boss's assumptions about you are evidenced especially by

- where you are placed in the company hierarchy. Are you a co-equal member of a team (Theory Y) or a subordinate member in a strict reporting order to a supervisor (Theory X)?
- how you receive work instructions. Are you involved as a participant in problem-solving and task development (Theory Y) or are you told precisely what you are to do and when (Theory X)?
- how you are urged to organize your time. Can you allocate your time according to your own work progress (Theory Y) or are you told how much time you must give to particular tasks (Theory X)?
- how you relate to other levels of decision-making in the company. Can you speak freely about ideas and concerns to any level of management (Theory Y) or must you always "go through channels" (Theory X)?
- how you perceive your work tasks in relation to the larger business mission of the company. Do you understand how your individual work contributes to the whole (Theory Y) or do you work largely in a vacuum, without much idea of the value of your contribution (Theory X)?

As a footnote, it must be said that even in the most liberal Theory Y organizations the principles of and techniques of Theory X management are occasionally employed. An uncommitted, immature employee may sometimes need to be told explicitly what to do and when. But even in such cases, the continued application of Theory X principles will not lead to the result the employee wants: a mature, contributing employee. For that result in the long term, the assumptions of Theory Y management are indispensable.

Also to be noted is the endemic philosophy of "paying dues" or enduring the "school of hard knocks" for new employees. The fact that an employee has risen in stature and maturity to enjoy liberalized Theory Y treatment in the company does not guarantee that he or she will provide that same treatment to incoming subordinates. Gender researchers have written widely about the "Queen Bee" syndrome. Whether applied to men or women, the syndrome suggests that once a person has attained a long-desired position of power and influence, he or she may be the worst taskmaster of subordinates seeking to rise in similar ways. The Golden Rule of treating others as you would be treated often seems to be forgotten among business leaders even in organizations most publicly committed to Theory Y management principles.

Management Tips

Theory X and Theory Y management techniques suggest very different motivational approaches for managers. Theory Y managers

1. ask employees what they think about business problems
2. encourage group discussion and evaluation
3. welcome tentative judgments and speculative ideas
4. thank employees for their efforts
5. trust employees to work toward company goals
6. free employees to develop individual skills for use within the organization
7. involve employees in the fair evaluation of their work
8. allow for the possibility of failure as an acceptable price for the value of experimentation.

For some people, this description of work life may seem hopelessly naïve. Yet, like Linda P., we each probably feel we could thrive in such a work climate. If we would choose a Theory Y management environment for ourselves, should we consider it too idealistic for others? That kind of double standard would bring us full circle back to the Rabble Hypothesis.

Key Six
Motivation by Reputation

The power and actions of a group can be explained by examining its components.

John F., 29, is a deed specialist with a large New England title company. He is single.

"Without bragging, I would describe myself as very popular among my coworkers, by which I mean the sixteen or so people who check on deeds and title claims all day. It's not exactly fascinating work, so we have this elaborate social stuff that goes on in the office. It's mostly a matter of funny comments to one another and occasional gags. But it makes the day pass faster.

"Most of us have been here at least three years, so we've been through a lot together: stolen cars, breakups in relationships, money problems, and the rest. But it has brought us all closer. I feel that some of my most loyal friends are the people I work with every day.

"It's almost humorous at times how close we are. Last month the company hired a new employee for our group, a guy we quickly came to call "the nerd"—he had absolutely no sense of humor. We didn't do anything in particular to make work life hard for him, but it was obvious that he just didn't fit in. Within a month he had quit. One of my friends here put it well: 'If you don't click, you gotta quit!'

"Another advantage of our closeness as a group is the whole matter of raises. The company awards pay raises on a merit system. But our group isn't eager to see one person get a bigger raise than someone else, so we have informally agreed on how many files we will each process during the day. No one goes above or below that number. Pay raises, consequently, are the same for everyone in the group. Our division manager knows that we have this self-imposed work limit, and she doesn't try to push any of us beyond it. She wouldn't have much luck trying.

"This was one aspect of work life that business school didn't prepare me for. A lot of days I feel like I'm back in the frat house—all for one and one for all."

Follow-up Information

In fact, John F. is among the least popular members of his work group. Behind his back, coworkers often mock his constant efforts to find playmates at work. John's supervisors privately rank him as doubtful for promotion. They are particularly concerned about his inability to complete assignments on time and his misuse of work time for social relations.

Motivators at Work

S.E. Asch conducted a memorable experiment that demonstrated the power of groups to motivate individual behavior. He placed a line on a display board. Beside it appeared three other lines, only one of which was the same length as the line set off by itself. Then Asch brought in groups of eight college students. Each student was asked in turn which of the three lines was the same length as the isolated line. Secretly, Asch had instructed seven of the students to give the same wrong answer. He wanted to discover how strong the influence of the group would be on the uninitiated eighth member. Would this student report what he or she saw to be true or would he or she go along with the obviously incorrect, but unanimous, answer of the rest of the group?

_____   A. _____
                                   B. _____
                                   C._____

The Asch Experiment: which line matches the original line in length?

As discovered that "one-third of all the estimates were errors identical with or in the direction of the distorted estimates of the majority."

This tendency of group members to lose their individual evaluative abilities is called "Groupthink" by social psychologist Irving Janis. Groups that want or need to be highly cohesive resist original thoughts and actions that may lead to disharmony or jealousy in the group. The result is often inaction or poor decision-making by group members. No one member wants to stand out for honor or for blame; to do so risks banishment from the group.

Most of the primary symptoms of Groupthink are probably present in John F.'s office. John has many reasons, both conscious and unconscious, for wanting to be a secure member of his work group. As one of the less competent employees, he needs the protection of the group to shield him from potential negative actions by management. If I'm "in" with the group, John reasons, the boss won't criticize me for fear of having a lot of people upset with him. In these thoughts, John is projecting onto the boss his own belief in the power of the group.

John also needs steady approval from the group. In the language of Alfred Adler, he "compensates" for his deep feelings of unworthiness and social unattractiveness by trying, ironically, to be the most social person in the office. He seeks the hour-by-hour approval of the group to assuage his painful feelings aroused by an "inferiority complex." John therefore turns almost every work interaction into an occasion for getting praise, approval, or just plain attention.

The group, however, has already begun to banish John, although so far without his knowledge. Why push out someone with such strong desires to be friendly? The group recognizes that John is self-seeking in his interactions; he wants something *from* the group, but not *for* the group. To that extent, he's quickly identified as a non-contributor to the welfare of the group and as a potentially dangerous member to the interests of the group.

Tenets of Groupthink:

Groupthink may be strong when members believe

- no one can resist the will of the group
- data in conflict with group information must be incorrect
- the group would not do the morally wrong thing
- nongroup members are inept, stupid, or weak
- all group members should wholeheartedly support one position
- if a person has private reservations, it's best to keep one's mouth shut
- there's probably no need to discuss topics in depth, since the group will quickly reach agreement
- information conflicting with group positions isn't worth hearing.

What will be John's eventual fate in the company? Management seems to have identified him already for the slow track—the one that leads out the door. As John begins to receive negative signals from management, he will no doubt carry them directly to the group: "You wouldn't believe what the manager put on my performance evaluation!" In one way or another, group members will communicate to John that they won't rally to his cause. In effect, he will learn where he really stands with the group. At this point, John will probably quit his job to seek a new and, he hopes, more supportive group with another company. John will no doubt explain to his new employer that "I got along great with my coworkers, but the manager just didn't like me. I don't know why. It was a personality conflict, I guess."

How Groups Work

George C. Homans describes group in terms of three interrelated elements:

Activities—Interactions—Sentiments

All workers in the group perform activities of some sort—writing reports, designing layouts, building products, and so forth. To accomplish these activities, workers must interact. And in the process of such interaction, workers develop a shared set of sentiments. Homans' central point is that a change in any one of these elements influences the other elements. In other words, the power and actions of the group can be explained by examining its components.

Let's say, for example, that the group develops strongly negative sentiments about salaries paid by the company. The interactions among members immediately change in character; group members begin to meet less for business purposes and more for "gripe sessions" to share opinions about the pay problem. Work activities slow dramatically as worker motivation falls off.

Or consider the spiraling effect that often leads to a highly cohesive group. In their initial interactions, workers find that they enjoy each other's company. Sentiments begin to warm. The positive change in this social element encourages even more interaction—which in turn increases sentiments. All the while, work activities may show little increase and may actually decrease. It's possible to have a highly social workplace where little actual work gets done.

Managing the Motivation of Groups

Almost by definition, managers are excluded from the tight bonds and trust of the group. No matter how politely the manager is treated by group members, he or she remains the primary threat to the cohesion and welfare of the group. The manager, after all, is the one who can physically separate the group by reassignment, destroy group unity by promotions and demotions, disturb group habits by giving new tasks, and disrupt group membership by hiring and firing. From the group's point of view, the manager is often the potential enemy.

The manager usually has full knowledge of the group's overt activities—the production line and work flow are easily observed. But the manager may know little about the group's private interactions and true sentiments. This information is carried by an informal but powerful channel of communication called the grapevine. In a recent survey of 10,000 employees, respondents were asked, "What are your major current sources of organizational information?" When asked to answer that question by choosing from fifteen categories, employees listed "immediate supervisor" first and "the grapevine" second.

Some managers, acting in response to "cognitive dissonance" (discussed in Key Three), do whatever they can to "tune out" the grapevine. They want to live with the illusion that workers are relatively content, that the opinions of management are respected as "law," and that business is operating normally. These managers usually make sure their offices are located far from the action of the workplace. They keep their doors closed, literally and symbolically. They eat with other managers, never with workers. In short, they believe that "what I don't know can't hurt me."

Unfortunately, these are usually the same managers who have no explanation when production schedules fall behind or when key workers quit.

Other managers try to listen to the rumblings carried by the grapevine. They cannot, of course, hear everything shared by group members communicating on the grapevine. Instead, the manager uses informal occasions during lunches and breaks as well as before and after meetings to listen. When the group senses that the manager is interested in the grapevine in a non-threatening way, the group often finds subtle ways of sharing particularly important rumors, questions, or concerns with the manager. Two or three group members may "have the manager's ear" without sacrificing their secure standing within the group.

Some managers have made the mistake of using the "bull in a china shop" approach to entering the employee grapevine. For example, a manager may spy on emails passed among employees in the office. Or a manager may call a meeting of all employees to "put an end to rumors." What such managers forget is that employees may continue to believe information from the grapevine and discount "announcement" information from the boss.

The key to successful interaction with the grapevine lies not in attempting to destroy it or undercutting its influence but instead in understanding what makes it popular, necessary, and credible for employees. If a manager understands why employees turn to the grapevine and why they believe it, he or she is well on the way to developing information methods and channels that compete well with grapevine information.

Management Tips

Groups exert powerful influence over the thoughts, feelings, and actions of group members. To harness some of the positive power of groups, managers should

1. Listen to the grapevine, especially when it carries distressing news.

2. Counteract false rumors and incorrect information
heard via the grapevine. The manager can use formal channels
of communication—the company newsletter, memos, email, and
meetings—to clarify facts and reduce apprehensions.

3. Structure group assignments and interactions to reduce
the negative influence of power cliques within the group.

Key Seven
Motivation by Self-Image

We are each the sum total of our life habits.

Helen R., 57, is publications assistant for a Detroit company that manufactures automobile seats. Her primary responsibility is to help produce a monthly e-newsletter and various company brochures, both on-line and in print. She lives alone with two cats.

"I don't often think of myself at all. I've had this job so long that I can't even find my resume anymore. If you asked my coworkers what I'm like, I think they would describe me as punctual and competent. I know the English language well and very few errors having to do with grammar, punctuation, or spelling ever creep into my work.

"I have pleasant working relations with others in the office. I'm often asked about my cats (I regularly update their pictures on my bulletin board). I keep a file of office birthdays and send out cards when they occur. I've done this for years for everyone from the president to the janitor. I think people appreciate it.

"As for my work life, there are no problems as far as I know. The newsletter hasn't received any complaints. My work has become easier since the manager sends me minutes of their meetings instead of having me actually attend these boring sessions. I can retire at 60, and I plan to work full-steam up to that point.

"I would describe myself as settled and comfortable. I have very few ups or downs, just life as usual each day. In the office, I've maintained some traditional practices, such as handwriting some shorter office memos and using my computer for email. I get teased for handwriting messages, but everyone in the office knows that it's just my way. They're not going to change me at this point. If it takes me a bit longer to get my work done, I just stay late at my own expense. It's my choice."

Follow-up Information

Helen R. grew up as the only daughter of a Presbyterian minister and his wife. Helen was praised for keeping her room neat and punished for boisterous play. At 17, Helen became pregnant and gave birth to a baby boy in an out-of-state church facility. At her father's insistence, the baby was privately put up for adoption. Helen returned to her parents' home, where she lived until their deaths a decade ago. Helen then took work as a secretary and gradually worked her way into her present position in publications. Helen likes regular schedules and repetitious tasks. She says that she cannot function at all during rush jobs and unexpected company crises. Her coworkers agree with her self-assessment.

Motivators at Work

What to do about Helen.… That's every manager's problem, for most larger offices have their Helens and Herberts: decent people with long service to the company but little usefulness.

Helen basic problem, of course, is that she is Helen. Co-workers say as much: "That's just Helen—not much you can do." In motivating Helen to new levels of achievement (or even previous levels of achievement), we first have to figure out how Helen became Helen.

The Process of Personality Formation

We are each the sum total of our life habits. Helen's personality, for example, is the result of 57 years of her own experimentation and evaluation. As a very young child, Helen may have experimented vocally by shouting or screaming. Her mother and father punished her. Helen learned not to shout or scream. She probably went on to experiment with ways of playing, ways of expressing anger, ways of showing off. In each case, her parents and teachers were significant forces in shaping Helen's eventual habits. Yes, Helen. No, Helen. Go to your room, Helen.

Without dragging Freud from his grave, it's probably safe to say that Helen's last important experiment in personal freedom involved the love affair that led to her pregnancy at 17. Her parents would not allow her to marry the young man or keep the baby. The whole matter was guarded within the family circle as a shameful tragedy for which Helen was to blame. Helen spent her twenties caring for aging parents—paying them back, in effect, for their "kindness" to her during her pregnancy and its emotional aftermath.

The Helen who sits before us now at 57 is the sum total of a life dedicated to self-doubt, self-denial, apology, and safety. She has learned in a thousand ways over the years that routine is good, that emergencies are bad, that simple tasks are comfortable, and that complex tasks are painful. Above all, she has come to feel that boredom is sanity and that excitement breeds disappointment.

Motivating Restricted Personalities

Some managers give up on the Helens in the office. Staff reductions are engineered in a way that cuts out their job descriptions. Transfers or early retirements are urged upon them, with the manager's reassurance that "it's best for you."

Fortunately, other managers refuse to push out people who know company operations well and have given years of their lives to company interests. Against all odds, these managers cherish the belief that Helen, even in her later years, can be motivated to succeed at new challenges. These are the managers who believe in "personality renaissance"—that our limitations (our "mind-forg'd manacles," in the poet Blake's phrase) are self-imposed and self-controlled. We can undo what we've done to ourselves and what has been done to us by others.

Thomas Harris, M.D., calls Helen's view of herself in relation to others her "life position." From an early age, Helen has come to think of herself as essentially "not OK"—she disobeyed Mom and Dad, she had an illegitimate child, and on and on. Other people, in Helen's view, are generally "OK." They seem so brave, so eager, so confident. In this "I'm not OK, you're OK" life position, Helen is more than content to perform the most routine, dreary tasks; she actually looks forward to stuffing envelopes and filing correspondence. In such simple tasks she runs no risk of having her not-OK status confirmed once again. The new and exciting tasks in the office can be left, she feels, for all those people who are OK.

Employees can assume any one of four life positions. Ideally, a coworker feels "I'm OK, you're OK. We are both secure enough to take on work challenges without fearing a devastating loss in self-esteem." Conversely, an employee can feel "I'm not OK, you're not OK." These are the people who despair not only for themselves but for the universe. "We have no chance for success. Let's just give up." Or a person can feel "I'm OK, you're not OK." These are the egotists who always know better, or believe they do. Interestingly, these types use night as a way of defining day, so to speak. They attempt to rise above the rest of us in their own view by putting us down. And, as we have seen in Helen's case, there are those who feel "I'm not OK, you're OK."

Each of our life positions can vary somewhat from day to day. But one position recurs more than any other, and it is this dominant position that defines our view of ourselves and way of relating to others.

What's a manager to do with an office full of "I'm not-OKs" or "you're not-OKs"? Some companies are fortunate to have counseling services available for particularly distressed personalities. But surely the hard work of psychological therapy is beyond the manager's job description and expertise. No manager can undo all of the effects of Helen's childhood and adolescence. Yet a manager must act in some way, especially when company goals are going unmet because of personality problems among the workers.

Perhaps the best option for manager is to take a chance and promote "OK-ness" among all employees. As Dr. Harris relates from his own practice, even the glimpse of "possible OK-ness" can spread like wildfire within the individual personality and eventually within the workplace.

Let's apply a healthy dose of "OK-ness" to Helen's case and monitor the result. Helen, as we have seen, doesn't want to leave behind her handwritten notes in an era of word-processing. She feels that by embracing modern technologies she will be setting herself up for another failure. She worries that "so many people in the office are already better than I am at word-processing—I'll never catch up." But enter "OK-ness" in the form of her supportive, good-natured boss. Instead of asking Helen to master new communication technologies, he simplifies her initial assignments to tasks such as creating an address list on the computer or basic spreadsheet. He chooses one of Helen's office friends to teach her what she needs to know to succeed at this task. The friend praises Helen often for her successes and makes light of failures. Gradually, Helen masters the skills involved in creating these projects. She expresses amazement at how much time the computer saves her in preparing and revising mailing labels and other data.

From this kind of simple beginning, Helen's personal renaissance begins. She learns other technological skills at home (her least threatening environment) and receives steady praise from her boss for the new skills she brings to the office. In time, people are commenting about "the new Helen," and relating to her in more positive ways. Her productivity and usefulness to the company increase dramatically.

Generalizing the "Helen" experience to the modern workforce, managers together with the company's training specialists must begin to develop a "ramp plan" for new employees, particularly those who have traditionally been passed over by American corporations. (Included here, for example, are women whose presence at entry levels jobs is enormous but whose place in the boardroom is still rare indeed.) A ramp plan is a series of staged work experiences likely to bring the new employee meaningful successes and rapid development within the organization. The ramp, of course, cannot be set too steeply—the employee would tend to slide back in discouragement. Nor can the ramp be set at too gradual an angle, for fear of boring or patronizing the employee.

Management Tips

Although managers cannot play the role of therapist to their employees, they can motivate improved performance in at least eight ways:

1. Treat employees as "OK" individuals.

2. Focus on the actions, not the person, when delivering negative evaluations.

3. Emphasize high hopes for each employee's professional growth.

4. Make development opportunities such as training seminars available to employees.

5. Promote team consciousness and resist scapegoating.

6. Praise employees for efforts and achievements.

7. Reward employees fairly.

8. Forgive and forget when these responses will contribute to employee development and company success.

A Final Note

Perhaps as a carryover from the American "just-take-a-pill" approach to physical ills, we may be tempted to think that an employee's psychological distress can be fixed by a single, heart-to-heart conversation or a visit or two to a company counselor.

Would that it were so. In reality, a manager has to prepare for a long undertaking in helping an employee clear away psychological obstacles to job performance. The success of that enterprise will be measured in small steps of improvement, not overnight transformation.

Key Eight

Motivation by Specific Goals

The actual process of developing work objectives begins at the highest organizational levels and then filters down.

Roger E., 37, works as an engineer for a St. Louis aerospace contractor. He is married with three children.

"I wish they would give me just one week to run this company. I would make one major change that would save thousands of hours of wasted labor and millions of dollars.

"I would just tell everyone what to do.

"It's just that simple, although my wife says my idea would appeal only to engineers. Everywhere in this company, about half of the workers know what needs to be done on projects and the other half don't. The uninformed sit at their desks inventing 'work' that makes no difference to anyone. Everyone gives the impression of working, of course.

"An aerospace project—a new shuttle engine, for example, let's say—is a massive undertaking involving hundreds of scientists, designers, engineers, technicians, and others. To keep from looking bad, these people will all busy themselves somehow during the work day; no one will go up to the boss and complain about nothing to do.

"But I guarantee you that at least half of these workers couldn't explain to you at a given moment exactly what they were trying to accomplish and how it served the larger interest of the project and the company. Many are doing activities or pursuing research for the sake of reports, which are filed with a manager and passed along to the company library. Paychecks arrive on time and that's that.

"I think a lot of workers yearn for more order and participation in their careers. I'd love a boss who just once would say to all of us in my work unit, 'Look, here's what the company is trying to accomplish. I'm going to give each of you a piece of the project and explain how it contributes to the company goal. Then I'll hold you accountable for your piece in the puzzle. The company is counting on you to do your part.'

"What we usually get, however, is something much more vague. You don't find out exactly what you were supposed to be doing until annual evaluations, when the boss blames you for not doing it. It comes down to 'Why didn't you tell me?,' 'But I did tell you!', and on and on.

"There would be a lot less frustration around here if each of us knew at the beginning of each day what we were supposed to accomplish that day. If we get it done well, we're on track for a raise or promotion. If we blow it, we get retrained or eventually fired. It's logical and it's fair. Why isn't it happening?"

Follow-up Information

In the fourteen years he has worked as an engineer, Roger
E. has undergone that same number of year-end performance
evaluations. In nine of those evaluations, Roger has scored high
in relation to his peers. He knows, however, that these evaluations have rarely been based on objective evidence of his work
effectiveness. Like many employees, Roger has perfected the art
of corporate appearance. He understands the behaviors that will
mark him as a "team player" and "valuable contributor" (phrases
used often by management). In playing the game of corporate
impressions, Roger doesn't consider himself any more phony than
his coworkers. He considers himself a skilled engineer. But he
does realize that his company has no meaningful way of defining
tasks and measuring employee effectiveness. The *de facto* system
within the company involves strategic friendship with management, name association with successful projects, and avoidance
of high-risk assignments. Roger E. has learned to play the game
well, but he doesn't like it.

Motivators at Work

Like many talented employees, Roger E. wants to be managed by objectives. That concept, usually abbreviated as MBO,
was introduced in America by Peter Drucker in the early 1950s
and popularized worldwide by George Odiorne, John Humble,
and others. In the 1980s, the MBO approach gained renewed
attention through the publication of best-selling books such the
The One-Minute Manager and *In Search of Excellence*. By the early
2000s, management by objectives had become the dominant

management style in hundreds of major corporations, including Purex, Tenneco, and Black & Decker.

At heart, MBO involves joint goal-setting between a superior and a subordinate. The manager or supervisor wants to distribute necessary work in such a way that employees are challenged to use their individual skills without feeling overwhelmed or under-utilized. The employees, similarly, want to negotiate an agreed-upon set of goals at which they can succeed, with reasonable effort.

Once clear goals have been established, the exact specification of tasks is often left to the employee, subject to managerial review. If the goal, for example, is the development of a site plan for a building, the company architect accepting that goal will not be told point-for-point how to go about developing the site plan. The architect's expertise is taken for granted.

Specific goals for various work units within a company must be arranged to fulfill general corporate goals. Although a manager may have substantial flexibility in determining which employee takes on particular goals, the manager usually does not have the option to alter or dismiss the major goals themselves. MBO negotiations, therefore, begin with the assumption that "someone in our group has to work toward this particular goal; the question is who's best for it."

When goals have been negotiated, they become the primary standard by which employee effectiveness is measured. In our earlier example, a company architect working toward the goal of developing a site plan agrees to produce approved renderings of that plan by a certain day. If that goal is accomplished on or before the deadline, the architect deserves company rewards (typically in the form of raises and promotion). If not, the architect may be in line for a variety of company demerits, including salary reduction or demotion.

MBO evaluation procedures, significantly, are behavior-based, not personality-based. When the company architect comes up for review, it is with the assurance that the performance evaluation won't be determined by such vague standards as "attitude toward work," "cooperation with others," and "interpersonal effectiveness." Instead, work performance will be primarily judged by one clear standard: were the agreed-upon goals met?

The actual process of developing work objectives begins at the highest organizational levels and then filters down to lower and lower levels in the organizational hierarchy. Because the process is cyclic in nature rather than linear, any significant change in specific goals at lower levels can eventually affect the redefinition of general goals at the highest organizational levels. In other words, the CEO may be driving the bus, but relying upon all the passengers to watch out for danger or better routes.

Management by objectives tends to fulfill employee's esteem and self-actualization needs (as explained in Key Two). Roger E. in our opening scenario isn't coming to work just to pick up a paycheck. He wants to apply his intelligence and training to interesting problems. As an expert in his field, he doesn't want a company executive to try to tell him precisely how to solve those problems. The executive, after all, probably knows much less than Roger about the matter. Roger wants to help determine clear goals, then be trusted to work out expert solutions. That trust on the part of the company breeds self-esteem and fulfillment for Roger. He feels loyal to his company because "I'm valued there."

Negotiating Performance Objectives

Much is at stake when a manager and a subordinate sit down to negotiate work goals. The manager's success depends upon distributing work goals clearly, fairly, and appropriately. The employee, too, faces risks: the goals accepted will be the standard by which later performance is evaluated. As one employee quipped to a manager, "you're asking me to pick the rope you'll later use to hang me."

The effective negotiation of work goals, therefore, usually takes time and involves five key points:

1. The goal itself: What does the company want done?

2. The goal qualifications: By what deadline must the goal be completed? Within what limits of quality control, inspection, or approval?

3. The available resources: What is the budget for achieving the goal? What personnel are available? What facilities, equipment, and supplies?

4. The standards of measurement: How will performance be measured? How often? By whom? How will measurement

results be communicated? What rewards are associated with successful performances?

5. The relative importance of the goal: What is at stake with regard to the goal? What visibility, risk, or responsibility comes with the goal?

Discussion of performance objectives usually focuses on all of these key issues. Some are more difficult to deal with than others, both for the manager and the subordinate. A salaried employee, for example, may opt for easier work goals if there's no incentive to accept more challenging assignments. In addition, the fear of failure for an individual may loom large in the case of high-visibility, high-risk goals. Even when potential payoffs are great, many employees tend to play it safe rather than risk the embarrassment of failure and company notoriety.

In negotiating performance objectives, therefore, a manager must present work goals in such a way that they seem not just financially or intellectually attractive but also organizationally safe. Especially when considering high-risk goals, an employee has a right to know "what happens if I fail?" The manager who has a reasonable answer to that question can often win employee commitment to risky work tasks.

As MBO programs have sprung up across industries, management researchers have been eager to learn how well this approach to employee motivation works. In general, MBO systems score high marks both from top management and employees. At Cypress Semiconductor Corporation, for example, the company's employees each commit to fulfilling particular goals by specified dates. A computer program tracks the status of these tasks and lets both management and the workforce know how work is proceeding. The result is what the company calls a "no excuses" work atmosphere: either the job gets done or it doesn't, with rewards passed out accordingly.

At the same time, the installation of MBO management practices in some companies has caused noticeable growing pains. First, employees used to doing whatever the boss asks can become more difficult to manage when given the opportunity to participate in goal-setting. Second, particular tasks can be linked too narrowly to specific rewards; thus, employees may develop a piecework attitude, devoting their attention to high-reward tasks and ignoring necessary, but low-reward work activities. Third, the workforce may spend too much time (and paperwork) getting ready to work rather than actually working. The discussion of goals may prove more expensive to the company than the achievement of those goals. Fourth, employees driven by their own assigned goals may become selfish to the detriment of the group. Employees may actually practice secretive or subversive behaviors with regard to the group so that their individual achievements stand out.

Most troublesome of all, report some MBO-oriented companies, is the "not-my-job-description" syndrome that nettles management-employee relations and often slows work to a crawl. In earlier union-dominated periods of American business and industry, each employee was assigned a carefully described job, whose terms were the result of considerable haggling between labor and management. Bosses were explicitly forbidden to require an employee to go beyond the limits of his or her job description, no matter what the emergency or opportunity at hand.

Ironically, that spirit of not-my-job has returned to some extent under the banner of MBOs. Employees may be unwilling to help out with tasks that they know will not be counted in the company's measuring system for rewards. To counteract this tendency, many companies have installed "fuzz" phrases in the list of objectives agreed to by the employee. A fuzz phrase is one that purposely lacks behavioral specificity and allows, instead, a broad range of interpretations and actions made necessary by changing markets and business needs. For example, one such objective might be worded as follows: "Employee demonstrates flexibility and creativity in helping to meet unexpected needs and crises in his or her work unit." That kind of language allows the company to reward the employee for going above and beyond the call of duty while also making it difficult for the employee to fall into the not-my-job-description syndrome. In companies that breed a whatever-it-takes attitude toward meeting customer needs, it's everyone's job to pitch in with tasks that may often lie well outside formal job descriptions. More than one top manager has helped stack boxes on shipping pallets to meet a crucial rush order.

These potential problems with MBO programs can be overcome by the MBO process itself. The desired form of organizational structures, reward systems, and employee interactions can all be stated as goals, then assigned appropriately throughout the organization. A manager, in other words, can be as responsible for how a group works as he or she is for how an engine works.

Management Tips

Management by objectives helps to solve the "who's-supposed-to-be-doing-what?" problem in business. MBO programs succeed when a manager

1. Takes time to discuss the context and importance of work goals with employees.

2. Negotiates goals for an individual employee based on that employee's skills, experience, and interest.

3. Ties performance evaluation directly to goals accepted by the employee.

4. Distributes rewards fairly according to goal fulfillment.

5. Monitors the success of goal-setting.

6. Uses results from goal-setting in redesigning organizational policies and procedures.

Key Nine
Motivation by Relationships

All people are involved in interpersonal trading or transacting.

Roberta K., 36, has worked as an accountant for seven companies in the past ten years. She is divorced and has one child, a teenage daughter.

"One question I always have to answer about my resume involves my frequent changes in employers. Those changes have all been by my choice. I've never had to leave a job because of the quality of my work.

"I do refuse, however, to work with childish people. I consider the office a place for adult, professional relationships. It's not a place for anger, pettiness, pouting, or shallow favoritism. Many of my most promising work experiences have turned out to be disappointing because of the maturity level of the people I work for or work with.

"As my strong recommendation letters make clear, I'm not an unreasonable or difficult person to work with. But I do expect to be addressed civilly by my supervisor. I expect my work instruction to be given to me in a timely way. I feel that I have the right to point out aspects of my work environment that prevent me from performing up to my standards. These are not unreasonable expectations.

"I don't believe that the office is the appropriate place to pursue or discuss one's social life. Therefore, I have kept my friendships separate from my career. Some of my coworkers may misunderstand my motives in this regard. I'm not unfriendly in the office, but I don't seek out nonwork-related conversation. I can't help but notice that some employees spend a large portion of the workday engaged in personal conversations, not work activities.

"I'm secure in my present position. My supervisor has complimented me on the accuracy and thoroughness of my work. She gives me accounting projects in sufficient time for the kind of careful job I insist on doing. I'm somewhat troubled, however, by her behavior in staff meetings. She seems to yield to the often unreasonable suggestions of some of her employees as a way of winning their favor. This aspect of her management style disappoints me, although I have not yet told her so. I wish she would be a strong leader."

Follow-up Information

Roberta is one of three sisters and the only one to complete college. She maintains frequent contact with her sisters, who often express their admiration for her professional accomplishments. Other than her sisters and a few church friends, Roberta has few social contacts. After a painful divorce, Roberta has had sole custody and financial responsibility for what she calls "a rebellious teenage daughter."

Roberta's financial life is problematic. She tends to exhaust her savings during periods of unemployment between jobs. For the past five years, she has suffered from alcoholism, a condition she hides from those outside her family and for which she has not sought professional help.

Motivators at Work

Getting the best out of people involves understanding them. But what is a manager to do with a stiff, uncooperative Roberta K.? Or, just as bad, with Charlie, the office clown? Or Samantha, the earth-mother who spends all day, every day seeking out and listening to everyone's domestic problems?

Although psychologist Eric Berne didn't direct his research toward business *per se*, his theories of Transactional Analysis (TA) have revolutionized the way managers observe and relate to their employees.

Berne suggests that all people are involved in interpersonal trading or transacting. When Roberta says, "Please don't disturb me" to Charlie, the office clown, she has initiated half of an interpersonal transaction. When Charlie responds, "You just can't take a joke, Roberta," he completes the transaction.

Transactions, according to Berne, spring from portions of our personalities over which we have only limited control. Each of us carries within three "speakers" or sub-personalities able to assert themselves: the parent, the adult, and the child.

The Parent

This personality force is the sum total of all the advice and commands we've been given over the years by various controllers, including parents, teachers, religious leaders, older siblings, and other authority figures. Although they may no longer be physically present, they are still "there" inside us, telling us (and others) what to do.

The Parent within us tends to rely upon unquestioned maxims and principles. Some of these may be deeply prejudicial: "You can't trust those kinds of people" (with regard to gender, race, religious, or national background) and "You can't teach an old dog new tricks" (with regard to age).

Other Parent messages within us may be reruns of messages instilled by our parents or other authority figures:

"Don't talk back."
"I'm only going to say this once."
"Do as you're told."
"I'm in charge here, not you."
"You don't want to get on my bad side."
"You'll be sorry if I have to get angry."
"If you lie to me, I'll never trust you again."

Although our Parent voice may not say such things so directly to business associates, we may communicate these essential messages in the way we react to others, particularly in moments of stress and crisis.

The Parent voice within can be viewed on a continuum from Nurturing (advice for the sake of growth) to Critical (advice for punishment). The Nurturing Parent communicates that bad actions may endanger the good person; the Critical Parent communicates that bad actions reveal the bad person.

In sum, the Parent portion of the personality emphasizes what should or must be done, as judged against a predetermined but often unexamined standard.

The Adult

The Adult portion of personality is reasonable and practical, but unemotional. The Adult examines causes, motives, and consequences of actions. The Adult makes plans, creates procedures, and functions within self-defined limits. The Adult takes responsibility for personal actions.

Roberta K., for example, is the consummate adult in her work behavior. She makes sure that each of her actions during the day is defensible by logical reasoning. She can explain exactly what she is doing, why, where, when, and for whom. She resists distraction from employees who do not have the same firm sense of purpose and direction. She leaves the employ of those companies where procedures and protocol are not maintained.

The Child

This final portion of the total personality is the source of emotional response. The Child casts aside logic and consequences in favor of spontaneity and natural feeling:

"This excites me!"
"It made me feel wonderful!"
"He really hurt my feelings."
"I like her style."
"I just enjoy working here."
"I'm getting really frustrated."
"I'm bored with my job."

The Child not only feels these emotions, but gives them high importance for determining follow-up actions. "I'm getting really frustrated...so I'm going to quit." "He really hurt my feelings...so I'll pay him back." "I like her style...so I'll promote her."

Like the Parent, the Child can be described as a continuum of internal forces ranging from the Happy Child to the Destructive Child. The Happy Child acts on the basis of personal feelings, but does so in a way that is not harmful to the interests of others. The Destructive Child also acts on the basis of personal feelings, but harms the interests of others in the process.

Unlike the Adult, the Child force does not stop to consider the causes, motives, or consequences before responding. Whether in joy or pain, the Child simply bursts out.

Parent-Adult-Child in Harmony

No one personality state in itself is ideal. The healthy personality allows all three internal forces to surface at appropriate times. We recognize these people as being "together."

These are the people who have a strong sense of values (Parent force) but at the same time can listen well to consider alternatives (Adult force). All the while, they're good company for their spontaneity, humor, and sympathy (Child force).

Motivating Parent-Dominated Employees

As described above, Parent-dominated people can be recognized by their reruns of unquestioned positions and prejudices. They may be proud of the fact that they dig in their heels when asked to do something they don't want to do. Or, by the same Parent force, they may feel an absolute duty to proceed with a task far beyond their abilities ("I should do this no matter what.").

Motivating this personality type always involves moving the person by degrees toward more Adult perceptions of the situation at hand. In the following dialogue between a manager and a Parent-dominated employee, notice how the manager emphasizes what *is* (Adult perception) to replace what *should be* (Critical Parent perception):

> Manager: "Jack, I'd like you to consider applying for the new government liaison position."
> Jack: "Thanks, but I'm not much for taking plunges. Better safe than sorry."
> Manager: "The new position would let you apply your many years of Pentagon experience."

Jack: "I'd rather let someone else try it first."

Manager: "I think you'd enjoy being in touch with top decision-makers here at the company and in government."

Jack: "Well..."

Manager: "And there's the pay. You could expect a significant raise."

Jack eventually decides to apply for the job as his manager highlights more and more of the reasonable attractions of the position from an Adult perspective. The manager would have had much less motivational success by opposing Jack's Parent tendencies: "Jack, you're always afraid to try something new. You should be more ambitious." In this approach, the manager is playing Critical Parent (what's wrong with Jack, what he should be). In so doing, the manager inadvertently magnifies Jack's own Parent responses: "Well, I think I should stick to what I know, not chase something new."

Motivating Adult-Dominated Employees

Like Mr. Spock on the original "Star Trek," Adult-dominated employees can be logical and reasonable to the point of their own disadvantage. Roberta K., for example, is such a good employee (by her definition) that she can hardly find a company worthy enough to employ her. Too often, the Roberta K.'s of corporate life end up as a footnote in an exit interview file: "Good performance potential, but poor interpersonal skills."

To motivate a Roberta to more human and more productive work relations with co-workers and clients, a manager must awaken her Child personality component. Roberta, it appears, has been reserving this Child aspect of personality for destructive, "let-go" drinking binges after work. She allows her Child to express itself outside of work, then reverts to a rigid form of Adult behavior for her work life.

In the following conversation with Roberta, a manager emphasizes and validates feelings, not logical responses. In time, Roberta may learn than her feelings are not only appropriate but are valued in the workplace. With that realization will undoubtedly come her own acceptance of the feelings of others:

> Manager: "I was disappointed to see that the Executive Committee canceled the marketing project you were working on. How did you feel about the situation
>
> Roberta: "I understood from their memo to me that the project had to be canceled because of regulatory changes." (Adult emphasis on reason)
>
> Manager: "I got a copy of the same memo. How did you feel when you read it?"
>
> Roberta: "I don't know all the facts, but I assume they made a logical decision."
>
> Manager: "But after all your work...To tell you the truth, I got really angry to see them change directions like this. How about you? (Discloses feelings, invites her feelings)
>
> Roberta: "Well, it did make me feel that I had wasted three weeks of work..."
>
> Manager: "That's entirely understandable."
>
> Roberta: "...and I was really frustrated that they didn't let me know sooner about regulatory changes. They had to know about them months ago!"
>
> Manager: "It's frustrating when top management isn't doing its job. I hate it when the left hand doesn't seem to know what the right hand is doing."

As this conversation proceeds, Roberta learns that she can share her work-related feelings, both positive and negative, with her manager. In time, she may broaden her network of work associates to include others she trusts with her feelings. One of these people may eventually help her take steps to control her alcoholism, a disease not unrelated to her suppressed Child responses.

Motivating Child-Dominated Employees

Finally, there's Charlie, the office clown—superbly gifted in social skills, but a time-waster for himself and for others. Acting from his inner Child, Charlie spends his entire day expressing his emotions and sympathizing with the emotions of others. It's hard to dislike Charlie—he's personable in the extreme. But likeability isn't the issue when work has to get done.

A manager probably won't have much luck approaching Charlie with strong Parent messages. The Child, after all, stands in rebellion against the Parent. Charlie behaves as he does to "get a little life into the office, put a bit of fun back in the day." There is little hope that Charlie will be motivated to more productive behavior by a series of "shoulds" in the form of a Parent message from his manager.

Instead, the manager tries in the following dialogue to move Charlie toward more Adult behavior. The manager's emphasis is on what is, without explicitly criticizing Charlie and specifying a list of "shoulds" for him.

> Manager: "I noticed your weekly report wasn't in by 10 a.m. yesterday."
>
> Charlie: "Oops. Barbara, Frank, and I got talking about the rumor that headquarters will be relocated to Toledo. Can you imagine that? The motto of that city is 'What's the point?'"
>
> Manager: "I got Barbara's and Frank's reports on time. I didn't get yours."
>
> Charlie: "Day late and a dollar short. My life story."
>
> Manager: "This isn't the first late report from you, Charlie. What's the problem?"
>
> Charlie: "No problems. Like I said, there are two kinds of time—company time and Charlie time."
>
> Manager: "I only pay attention to company time. What keeps you from getting your work in on time?"
>
> Charlie: "Nothing in particular. Just day-to-day stuff, I guess."
>
> Manager: "Such as?"

As this conversation proceeds, Charlie is forced off his routine of one-liners and other jokes to confront his Child behavior and its results. The manager at no time lectures Charlie on what should be done; instead, the emphasis is on what is happening and what may be causing it. Charlie the Child may be ready to rebel against and reject the Parent forces, but he is ill-armed to refute the Adult facts of his work life. With persistence on the manager's part, Charlie can regain his usefulness as an employee without losing his charm as a person.

As with most catchy ways of describing human personality, the Parent-Adult-Child pattern can be applied too simplistically by many well-intentioned managers. It is important not to label individuals in your organization as any one personality type; in fact, we each exhibit a complex interaction of the Parent-Adult-Child forces in our daily work and private lives. Furthermore, a manager must be ready to see and respond to sudden changes in employee behavior. An employee who has tended to operate from the Parent position may, especially in times of crisis, exhibit all the characteristics of the Child.

Finally, managers owe it to themselves to reflect upon their own conflicting inner motives and needs. Often our frustration with those who work for us stems directly from our misunderstanding of what we need and want from those individuals. In short, one of the best ways to get to know the Parents, Adults, and Children around us is to get to know these forces within ourselves.

Management Tips

Employees exhibiting Parent, Adult, or Child behavior in the workplace can be motivated to more productive work habits in three primary ways:

1. Parent-dominated employees resist original thinking and perpetuate stereotypes in their work and relationships. Use Adult rationality and logic to persuade such people that their limitations of self and others are both unnecessary and disadvantageous.

2. Adult-dominated employees lose the zest of work challenges and perform poorly in groups. Demonstrate to such people that feelings, appropriately expressed, are natural and valuable in the workplace.

3. Child-dominated employees base their actions primarily on feeling. Showing them what they should be doing (Parent perspective) is often less effective than pointing out the actual results of their behavior.

Key Ten

Motivations by the Games People Play

Psychological games waste the energies of well-intentioned employees.

In the following dialogue, a supervisor talks with Ralph C., 24, an account executive responsible for a major fast food advertising account.

> Ralph: "As I told you before, I'm under a lot of pressure from Burger Boys. They want their ads right up there with the national chains."
>
> Supervisor: "They want TV ads?"
>
> Ralph: "Yes, but I just finished buttoning up the big print ad campaign for them—you know, the Better Burger ads. What are we supposed to do, just trash that hard work?"
>
> Supervisor: "I guess that depends on what the client is willing to pay for."
>
> Ralph: "Yes, but they haven't even given the print campaign a chance to work."
>
> Supervisor: "Have you discussed this with them, Ralph?"
>
> Ralph: "Yes, I've tried on several occasions, but all they can talk about is television advertising."

Supervisor: "Well, it seems obvious to me that your client wants some leadership from you on a new kind of ad campaign for television."

Ralph: "Yes, but how do I get them to give the print ads a chance to work?"

Supervisor: "I guess that's your call, Ralph. I don't seem to be helping very much."

Follow-up Information

Ralph C. comes from a family of very successful professionals. His mother is a prominent neurologist, his father an attorney. Brad, Ralph's older brother, is a regional director for the Environmental Protection Agency.

Ralph's mother and father convinced Ralph at an early age that he was no Brad. In high school and college, Ralph's test scores and grades were well below Brad's. Ralph struggled for his B.A.; Brad breezed through an MBA at Wharton. It went on and on. Brad owned his home, Ralph rented; Brad married Ms. Perfect, Ralph was dating on and off; Brad drove a Porsche, Ralph a old Toyota.

Ralph had the unshakeable feeling that a dark cloud seemed to move wherever he moved. He had come to expect it at the most important moments of his personal life and career. The Better Burger print campaign was his first big project in advertising. But right on schedule, the dark cloud had moved in. The clients wanted to change to television ads.

Motivators at Work

Most of us probably participated in a childhood game, "Bug the Sub," when a substitute teacher took over class for the day. Game behaviors were predictable for our uproarious classmates, and total scoring depended on the outcome by the end of the day: highest points for the substitute's hysterical tears, less for harangues, calls for the principal's assistance, and threats to call parents.

For some of us, the playing of psychological games didn't end with elementary school. We may still have routine behaviors or games that, consciously or subconsciously, we play out in our business lives.

In the opening scenario, Ralph is playing one of the most familiar of such games: "Yes, but." Like all psychological games, "Yes, but" has three characteristics:

1. The moves are ritualized and repetitious on the part of the game initiator. No matter what the supervisor says, Ralph will respond with an explanation beginning with "Yes, but."

2. The game has a surface level and a hidden level. At the surface level, Ralph seems sincere in his request for his supervisor's advice. But at a hidden level, the game is already decided. Ralph will accept none of his supervisor's ideas and, in fact, is not even interested in those ideas.

3. The game empowers the initiator by frustrating the other player. Ralph draws his game victory not from the value of his

supervisor's advice but from the supervisor's eventual inability to offer advice. Ralph "proves" his position to be correct by defeating the other person's efforts to help. In transactional terms (as explained in Key Nine), Ralph the Child overpowers the Supervisor Parent by reducing him to silence. (A similar behavior can be observed in the child who screams "I want it!" over and over until the parent quits objecting and just gives in.)

Psychological games waste the energies of well-intentioned employees. Ralph's supervisor, for example, didn't recognize that he was caught up in a psychological game. He worked hard, therefore, to come up with alternatives, explanations, and possibilities for Ralph to consider. The supervisor didn't understand that the goal of the game, for Ralph, was achieving frustration, not helpfulness. In many companies, psychological games on the part of key employees lead to unnecessary meetings, memos, emails, letters, and reports—all wasted.

Just as harmful, however, are the effects of psychological gaming on the game player himself. In our opening scenario, Ralph is rehearsing once again a game pattern he has played since childhood. Psychologists believe, in fact, that lifelong psychological games usually begin in childhood. Success breeds success, and with each repetition of his "Yes, but" game Ralph becomes more and more a master of its techniques. He learns, that is, how to initiate the game so subtly that not even his closest associates realize they are caught in a no-win situation until it is too late.

In time, therefore, game players become increasingly dangerous to their organizations. The same games that block conversation can end up blocking production schedules and development plans. The size of a game player's "win," after all, is in direct relation to the total amount of frustration he produces.

Recognizing Psychological Games at Work

Managers who attempt to motivate their employees by the various methods described in these chapters may sometimes find even their most intensive efforts backfiring. The culprit may be a psychological game. Recognize its presence by the game player's recurring behaviors that suggest a no-win course for your efforts. The sooner you spot this no-win horizon, the sooner you can redirect your effort to end the game and seek better solutions.

Motivating Psychological Game-Players

The essence of the psychological game lies in the player's need to frustrate you. Understanding the nature of that perverse need is the first step for motivating the game player to more productive interaction.

Game-players usually have a long history of unsuccessful relations with authority figures. In some cases, an authority figure always imposed his or her will. In other cases, the authority figure withheld desired respect and affection.

The game-player, because he cannot get what he wants from the authority figure, must psychologically remove the authority figure's importance. In game-playing conversations, this can best be accomplished by reducing the authority figure to frustrated silence (the direct opposite, that is, of authoritative speaking). In game-playing actions, the goals of the organization are subverted by apparently innocent delays, misplaced documents, suspicious equipment breakdowns, and ambiguous directions.

A manager cannot literally give in to a game-player's attempts to psychologically assassinate authority figures in the company. But a manager can supply in a positive way what the game-player seeks in a negative way. In other words, a manager can help a game-player find enough self-importance and recognition so that game-playing becomes unnecessary.

In the opening scenario, for example, Ralph's supervisor could have realized early on that Ralph would say "yes, but" to all his suggestions. Instead of playing Ralph's game, the supervisor could have gone directly to the heart of Ralph's problem: his perceived lack of recognition and success, in this case regarding the print ad campaign he has worked hard on.

Notice in this revised conversation how the supervisor avoids Ralph's unproductive psychological game and at the same time motivates him to new levels of achievement:

> Ralph: "As I told you before, I'm under a lot of pressure from Burger Boys. They want their ads right up there with the national chains."
> Supervisor: "They want TV ads?"
> Ralph: "Yes, but I just finished buttoning up the big print ad campaign for them—you know, the Better Burger ads. What are we supposed to do, just trash that hard work?"

Supervisor (recognizing the beginning of the "yes, but" game): "Ralph, let's stop right here. What's really bothering you about the Burger Boys account?"

Ralph: "What do you mean?"

Supervisor: "How do you feel about the whole matter?"

Ralph: "Kind of kicked around, I guess."

Supervisor: "Kicked around?"

Ralph: "Yeah, I do my best for these guys, and they pull the rug out from under me. I thought I could trust them."

Supervisor: "So what would make you feel better about things?"

Ralph: "I have no idea."

Supervisor: "Come on, Ralph. You said this whole thing made you feel lousy. So what would make you feel better?"

Ralph: "It sounds stupid, but at this point I'd love to get revenge. See them stuck without any ad campaign at all."

Supervisor: "And how does that help you?"

Ralph: "Well, it doesn't help me financially, but it would sure make me feel they got what they deserve."

Supervisor: "So there's your choice, Ralph. You can go on resisting their desire for TV ads and get your revenge. Or you can skip the revenge and succeed financially, both for yourself and the company.

Ralph (laughs): "The revenge is tempting, but I'd rather have the money, I guess. I'll talk to them about television ads."

The supervisor concludes by praising Ralph's choice and reminding him how valuable his work is for the company.

Not all psychological game-playing in business is negative. It may be psychologically healthy, for example, for many salespeople to think of their daily work as "the game" and to participate in friendly in-house contests for top sales. Rejection and disrespect from clients can then be interpreted as "just part of the game" rather than as ego-threatening attacks. Temporary workers and those managers who have developed portable careers inevitably look upon each of their relatively short job stays as moves on the checkerboard of getting ahead. The idea of work life as a fascinating game, in other words, can be beneficial for many employees.

A Final Note

We should not look upon psychological game-players as sociopaths or social pariahs. To some extent, we all engage in some forms of manipulative game behavior in our personal and professional lives. What we should watch for in ourselves and in others is that point at which psychological games become personally and organizationally destructive. Then the game's over—or should be.

Management Tips

By adulthood, some people have become masters at elaborate psychological games intended to make the game partner feel frustrated, helpless, guilty, or insignificant. Managers can avoid the dangerous effects of game-playing in their organization in these ways:

1. Recognize psychological games by their repetitious patterns on the part of the game-player and the no-win future for the game partner.

2. Remove the game-player from key roles where his actions can subvert organizational goals.

3. Motivate the game-player to more productive behavior by providing in a positive way the attention, recognition, or understanding he perversely seeks through negative games.

Conclusion

With hiring and training costs rising precipitously in most companies, there has never been a better time to get the most from the employees you have. Motivating these people, as we have seen, begins with a single principle: understanding the needs of the individual you seek to motivate.

You may be surprised to find how inexpensive such motivation can be within your organization. A supportive comment to the right person at the right time costs you little, yet may pay extraordinary dividends in terms of employee productivity and loyalty to the company. It is important to experiment freely and regularly with the motivators described here. These are powerful tools that can literally transform lackluster workers into company leaders.

Using scenarios, we have seen how different individuals respond to quite different motivators. Gathered here for ease of reference are the abbreviated versions of the specific Management

Tips offered at the end of each chapter. Put these suggestions where they belong—at work for you!

Summary of Management Tips

Key One

Motivation by Expectation

Expectancy theories of motivation emphasize the internal world of hopes and dreams more than the external world of money and position. Four practical lessons can be drawn from the Todd M. case:

1. Each individual has his or her own set of expectations and beliefs regarding work. These inner forces are their prime motivators for achievement.

2. Managers should not assume that external symbols of value (a high salary, a company car, and so forth) automatically have personal motivating value for a particular employee.

3. Managers choose motivators based on their knowledge of employees' personal expectations.

4. Managers guard against fall-offs in motivation particularly at the beginning of unpromising tasks and toward the conclusion of sure-bet tasks.

Key Two

Motivation by Understanding What Others Need

Several insights for managers emerge from an understanding of the hierarchy of needs.

1. Motivators have meaning only in relation to the strength of a given need as perceived by the individual employee. At some stages, the lure of money may be almost meaningless; at other stages, it may seem all-important.

2. Managers can understand their employees' needs only by listening to and observing them.

3. Employees will take on new challenges only when their other needs remain relatively satisfied. The increased status of new job responsibilities and titles may be unattractive to employees concerned primarily about social relations.

4. Managers tend to project their own stage of need onto their employees. A manager obsessed with upper levels of self-actualization, for example, may not understand why subordinates resist attending a two-week seminar on advanced technical

skills. Don't they want to be more competent than their coworkers? Don't they want to master sophisticated skills? Perhaps not, at least from the point of view of the workers themselves. These opportunities may be motivating for managers who have already satisfied other levels of need, but not for subordinates who are still struggling to satisfy those needs.

Key Three

Motivation by Fairness

Managers sometimes cause inequities by the way they distribute work and rewards. But just as often, as in the Peggy W. case, inequities develop as a result of worker attitudes and actions. No matter what the cause, perceived inequities can be minimized in these ways:

1. Managers should study their organizations to determine where equity comparisons are likely to be made.

2. Managers can influence equity comparisons by distinguishing job titles, job descriptions, chains of reporting, numbers of people supervised, and types of rewards (including "perks") distributed.

3. Managers can prevent some forms of equity comparison by restricting the amount or type of information available to employees about the total amount of work and rewards given to others.

4. Managers can reduce the negative impact of unavoidable inequities (as perceived) by the ethical use of expectation motivators. Employees who feel cheated in the short term may continue to work hard toward company goals if they have reasonable expectations of just rewards in the long term.

Key Four
Motivation by Work Attitudes

A clear understanding of the differences between motivators and maintenance factors helps managers select powerful motivators that connect with worker needs and desires.

1. In assessing motivational programs, managers should watch for the Hawthorne Effect. Any employee or group of employees highlighted for special attention will respond with temporarily increased productivity.

2. Dissatisfying work conditions can restrict the capacity of workers to perform and their motivation to do so.

3. The elimination of dissatisfying work factors does not automatically create a satisfying and motivating work climate.

4. Motivators (satisfiers) may be different for each individual. Managers have to understand an individual worker's wants in order to choose effective motivators.

5. Managers often have a set of motivators for themselves that differ significantly in priority from those of their workers. Managers should not impose their motivational priorities on others who may have quite different motivational needs.

Key Five

Motivation by Approval

Theory X and Theory Y management techniques suggest very different motivational approaches for managers. Theory Y managers

1. ask employees what they think about business problems
2. encourage group discussion and evaluation
3. welcome tentative judgments and speculative ideas
4. thank employees for their efforts
5. trust employees to work toward company goals
6. free employees to develop individual skills for use within the organization
7. involve employees in the fair evaluation of their work
8. allow for the possibility of failure as an acceptable price for the value of experimentation.

Key Six
Motivation by Reputation

Groups exert powerful influence over the thoughts, feelings, and actions of group members. To harness some of the positive power of groups, managers should

1. Listen to the grapevine, especially when it carries distressing news.

2. Counteract false rumors and incorrect information heard via the grapevine. The manager can use formal channels of communication—the company newsletter, memos, email, and meetings—to clarify facts and reduce apprehensions.

3. Structure group assignments and interactions to reduce the negative influence of power cliques within the group.

Key Seven

Motivation by Self-image

Although managers cannot play the role of therapist to their employees, they can motivate improved performance in at least eight ways:

1. Treat employees as "OK" individuals.

2. Focus on the actions, not the person, when delivering negative evaluations.

3. Emphasize high hopes for each employee's professional growth.

4. Make development opportunities such as training seminars available to employees.

5. Promote team consciousness and resist scapegoating.

6. Praise employees for efforts and achievements.

7. Reward employees fairly.

8. Forgive and forget when these responses will contribute to employee development and company success.

Key Eight
Motivation by Specific Goals

Management by objectives helps to solve the "who's-supposed-to-be-doing-what?" problem in business. MBO programs succeed when a manager

1. Takes time to discuss the context and importance of work goals with employees.

2. Negotiates goals for an individual employee based on that employee's skills, experience, and interest.

3. Ties performance evaluation directly to goals accepted by the employee.

4. Distributes rewards fairly according to goal fulfillment.

5. Monitors the success of goal-setting.

6. Uses results from goal-setting in redesigning organizational policies and procedures.

Key Nine
Motivation by Relationships

Employees exhibiting Parent, Adult, or Child behavior in the workplace can be motivated to more productive work habits.

1. Parent-dominated employees resist original thinking and perpetuate stereotypes in their work and relationships. Use Adult rationality and logic to persuade such people that their limitations of self and others are both unnecessary and disadvantageous.

2. Adult-dominated employees lose the zest of work challenges and perform poorly in groups. Demonstrate to such people that feelings, appropriately expressed, are natural and valuable in the workplace.

3. Child-dominated employees base their actions primarily on feeling. Showing them what they should be doing (Parent perspective) is often less effective than pointing out the actual results of their behavior.

Key Ten

Motivation by the Games People Play

By adulthood, some people have become masters at elaborate psychological games intended to make the game partner feel frustrated, helpless, guilty, or insignificant. Managers can avoid the dangerous effects of game-playing in their organization in these ways:

1. Recognize psychological games by their repetitious patterns on the part of the game-player and the no-win future for the game partner.

2. Remove the game-player from key roles where his actions can subvert organizational goals.

3. Motivate the game-player to more productive behavior by providing in a positive way the attention, recognition, or understanding he perversely seeks through negative games.

On-line Resources

www.motivationquotes.com
A plethora of motivational and inspirational quotes.

www.woopidoo.com/business_quotes/
Motivational business quotes from business experts, financial authorities, and authors on business and leadership topics.

www.solveyourproblem.com/
Motivational quotes for business and work to provide a "pick-me-up" for employees and even management.

www.motivationalinterview.org/
Resources on motivational interviewing, including general information links, discussion board, training resources, and information on reprints.

www.casaa.unm.edu/mi.html
A site explaining motivational interviewing as a client-centered, directive method for facilitating change by helping people explore and work through interactive techniques.

www.pickthebrain.com/blog/21-proven-motivation-tactics/
Presents 21 tactics to help you maximize motivation in yourself and others.

www.motivation123.com
Articles and tips on motivation, inspiration, and finding happiness. Checklists, quotations, and free ideas kit.

www.accel-team.com/motivation/index.html
A site focusing on employee motivation, the organizational environment, and productivity.

www.alleydog.com/101notes/mot-emot.html
Psychology class notes for the Psychology of Motivation and Emotion, created by a psychology instructor for psychology students.

www.healthtree.com/articles/motivation/science.php
This site discusses the science and psychology of motivation, disincentives, role of positive motivation, and motivation theory.

www.psychology.org/links/Environment.../Motivation/
Resources on the motivations and drives that influence behavior.

www.vanguard.edu/faculty/ddegelman/.../index.aspx?doc_id
Resources on motivational theories, beliefs, goals, and research on motivation and emotion.

www.psychology.about.com/od/leadership/p/leadtheories.htm
Presents theories of leadership in relation to their motivational strategies and effects. Eight major leadership theories are treated here.

Suggested Readings

Baldoni, John. Great Motivation Secrets of Great Leaders. New York: McGraw-Hill, 2004.

Barrier, Michael. "Improving Worker Performance," Nation's Business, September 1996, p. 28.

Beck, Robert C. Motivation: Theories and Principles. 5th ed. Englewood Cliffs, NJ: Prentice Hall, 2003.

Bernardin, H. John and Richard W. Beatty. Performance Appraisal: Assessing Human Behavior at Work. Boston: Kent Publishing Company, 1984.

Champagne, Paul J. Motivation Strategies for Performance and Productivity: A Guide to Human Resource Development. New York: Quorum Books, 1989.

Chandler, Steve. 100 Ways to Motivate Yourself. Franklin Lakes, NJ: Career Press, 2004.

Cheng, Yuan and Arne L. Kelleberg. "Employee Job Performance in Britain and the United States," Sociology, February 1996, p. 115.

Cherrington, David J. Organizational Behavior: Management of Individual and Organizational Performance. Boston: Allyn and Bacon, 1989.

Cottrell, David. Monday Morning Motivation: Five Steps to Energize Your Team, Customers, and Profits. New York: HarperBusiness, 2009.

Deckers, Lambert. Motivation: Biological, Psychological, and Environmental. New York: Allyn & Bacon, 2009.

Durand, David. Perpetual Motivation: How to Light Your Fire and Keep It Burning in Your Career and in Life. New York: Crossroad Publishing, 2006.

Eliot, Andrew J. and Carol S. Dweck. Handbook of Competence and Motivation. New York: Guilford Press, 2007.

Govern, John M. Motivation: Theory, Research, and Applications. New York: Wadsworth, 2003.

Hersey, Paul and Kenneth H. Blanchard. Management of Organizational Behavior: Utilizing Human Resources, 5th ed. Englewood Cliffs, NJ: Prentice Hall, 1988.

Herzberg, Frederick, Bernard Mausner, and Barbara Snyderman. The Motivation to Work. New York: John Wiley, 1959.

Higgens, James M. The Management Challenge: an Introduction to Management. New York: Macmillan, 1991.

Johnson, Jim. The Sixty-Second Motivator. New York: Dog Ear Publishing, 2006.

Kotter, John P. "Kill Complacency," Fortune, August 5, 1996, p. 168.

Kovach, Kenneth A. "What Motivates Employees? Workers and Supervisors Give Different Answers," Business Horizons, September-October 1987, pp. 58-65.

Lavole, Richard D. The Motivation Breakthrough: 6 Secrets to Turning On the Tuned-Out Child. New York: Touchstone, 2008.

Lawler, Edward E. Motivation in Work Organizations. Monterey: Brooks/Cole Publishing Company, 1963.

Lowe, Tamara and Rudolph Giuliani. Get Motivated! New York: Broadway Business, 2009.

Maslow, Abraham H. Motivation and Personality. 2nd ed. New York: Harper & Row, 1970.

Macarov, David. Incentives to Work. San Francisco: Jossey-Bass, 1970.

McClelland, David. The Achieving Society. New York: Van Nostrand Reinhold, 1961.

McNerney, Donald J. "Employee Motivation: Creating a Motivated Workforce," HR Focus, August 1996, p. 1.

Morf, Martin. Optimizing Work Performance: A Look Beyond the Bottom Line. New York: Quorum Books, 1986.

Murrell, Hywell. Motivation at Work. London: Methuen, 1976.

Nadler, David A. and Edward L. Lawler. "Motivation: A Diagnostic Approach," in J. Richard, Edward E. Lawler, and Lyman W. Porter, eds. Perspectives on Behavior in Organizations, 2nd ed. New York: McGraw-Hill, 1983, pp. 67-78.

Pinder, Craig C. Work Motivation: Theories, Issues, and Applications. Glenview: Scott, Foresman, 1984.

Pink, Daniel. Drive: The Surprising Truth About What Motivates Us. New York: Riverhead, 2009

Quick, Thomas L. Quick Solutions: 500 People Problems Managers Face & How to Solve Them. New York: John Wiley & Sons, 1987.

Reeve, John Marshall. Understanding Motivation and Emotion. New York: Wiley, 2008.

Robins, Stephen P. Management. Englewood Cliffs, NJ: Prentice Hall, 1991.

Shah, James Y. and Wendi L. Gardner. Handbook of Motivation Science. New York: Guilford Press, 2007.

Steers, Richard. Motivation and Work Behavior. New York: McGraw-Hill, 1983.

Thomas, Kenneth Wayne. Intrinsic Motivation at Work: Building Energy and Commitment. New York: Berrett-Koehler Publishers, 2002.

Tulgan, Bruce. "Managing Generation X," HR Focus, November 1995, p. 22.

Vroom, Victor H. Work and Motivation. New York: John Wiley, 1964.

Wlodkowski, Raymond J. Enhancing Adult Motivation to Learn: A Comprehensive Guide for Teaching All Adult. San Francisco: Jossey-Bass, 2008.

Yukl, Gary. Skills for Managers and Leaders. Englewood Cliffs, NJ: Prentice Hall, 1990.

Zaleznik, Abraham. The Motivation, Productivity and Satisfaction of Workers: a Prediction Study. Boston: Harvard University, Division of Research, Graduate School of Business Administration, 1954.

www.ingramcontent.com/pod-product-compliance
Lightning Source LLC
Chambersburg PA
CBHW051838020726
47502CB00005B/1854